To
Book Club's

RBSheffield

Nov 1997

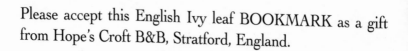

Please accept this English Ivy leaf BOOKMARK as a gift from Hope's Croft B&B, Stratford, England.

Other Publications by R.D. Stafford

The Funeral Club
A Novel

Shades of Gray
A Play

"The Struggle for Creative Control of Play Productions:
Interviews with Arthur Miller, Edward Albee, Adrian Hall,
and Frank Rich," in *Theatre Southwest*.

"Who Owns It? Personal Interviews with Arthur Miller
and A.J. Antoon," in *Southern Theatre*.

Summer at Hope's Croft

Richard D. Stafford

SF COMMUNICATIONS

TEXAS * GEORGIA

SF COMMUNICATIONS INC.
P.O. Box 8
Demorest, Georgia 30535
1-800-357-6301

Copyright © 1997 by SF Communications, Inc.

Front and back cover art renderings by Chris Bazley, Gloucestershire, England.

Front and back cover design by Bill Stratton, Digital Impact Design, Cornelia, Georgia.

Graphic Designers, Don Bagwell, Sara Zimmerman, Jason Pritchett and Jason Blackburn.

Library of Congress Catalogue Number TX 4-299-140

ISBN # 0-9650478-1-4

Stafford, Richard D., 1951

First Printing, October 1997

1 2 3 4 5 6 7 8 9

PRINTED AND MANUFACTURED IN THE UNITED STATES

U.S.A. $ 11.95
CAN $ 14.95

For
Chris and Angie
Alderminster Farm B&B
Stratford upon Avon
Warwickshire, England

C H A P T E R   O N E

The Zepino's frozen pizza lacked character. Wasn't much more than old cardboard, garnished with imitation everything. Oh yes, it was a combination pizza all right, a combination of #3 red-dye colored tomatoes, soy bean sausage, and boring crust that sat apathetically on my plate. I took one last bite and chewed persistently on a non-flexible, leathery pepperoni which finally clung unforgivingly in my throat. The meal was choking me; it might as well have been roofing shingles, served half frozen —half too hot — from the microwave oven, a garage sale bargain I had bought years earlier as a gift to myself... a laboring steel worker. It was purchased in celebration of Ronald Reagan's departure from the White House. The tip of my tongue kept massaging a tiny spot on the roof of my mouth where the flesh had been burned away from an unexpected dab of pizza which was near nuclear fission temperature. The irritating burn made me temporarily forget that it was my birthday, my forty-ninth birthday, alone in my dismal Bethlehem, Pennsylvania apartment.

Chucking the remaining slices of the quick-fix, Americanized Italian meal in the overflowing living room trash can, I caught a glimpse of a package delivery truck pulling up just outside my place. The patriotic looking truck stopped with a jerk after slipping through the thickly polluted air which tinted the morning sky a faded gray. Out on the damp cement stoop, an ugly metal pole supported a scraggly morning glory vine which grew timidly, with only a few half-opened buds, each struggling against the polluted oxygen it breathed. Like me, I suppose, they were dwarfed and unable to fully open, suppressed by a lack of nourishing food and fresh clean air.

Dressed in her officious uniform, the middle-aged delivery clerk bounced to my door and fingered the black door buzzer. I wondered why she was buzzing my door and considered not answering the late Saturday morning summons.

"After all, who would be sending me an urgent message?" I contemplated.

Another persistent, even irritating buzz.

"Perhaps some birthday surprise, from an old forgotten friend to cheer up the passing of nearly half-a-century of life…well, existence?"

Squinting through the peep hole, the only opening in the heavily nicked metal clad door, I turned the chrome knob, released the dead bolt, and opened to a clipboard awaiting the signature of my name, Nathan Bradbury. I obliged the woman, received an overnight envelope, and shut the door steadfastly against the encroaching day.

The thin cardboard carrier seemed to hold only a letter, it wasn't a birthday package at all. In frisbee fashion I tossed the red, white, and blue envelope to the well-worn sofa and strolled quickly back to the tiny kitchen for a cola to clear the pepperoni. All three of my drinking glasses were in the sink, unwashed, so I popped the top of the red and white can and headed straight back to the saggy couch, an inheritance from my mom shortly before her death in 1990, and the same sofa I napped on as a kid in the late 40's, now reupholstered for the umpteenth time.

I lifted cheap drug store reading glasses to my eyes and read the mailing label aloud for only me to hear:

"Nathan Bradbury
723 1/2 Winston Avenue
Bethlehem, Pennsylvania   18071

Let's see, return address, uhm…

John Hall, Legal Counsel
800 Rother St.
Stratford, England CV378AX," shaking my head, still puzzled.

"Who is John Hall?" I questioned, wondering what trouble was about to land on my plate. Another long sip of cola. I placed the envelope on the coffee table, glasses on top, and leaned back against the latest corduroy covering. "Stratford?"

My grandparents had lived near Stratford for most of their lives, Ilmington to be exact. The last time I had heard from them was when my mother died. From a nursing home in Stratford, a note had been sent acknowledging my mother's passing and conveying sorrow. The note was sent by a nurse since, I suppose, my grandparents were both too infirm to even be aware of their daughter's death. As I sat there on the dark brown sofa, long lost magical images of my grandparents' home drifted into my consciousness. Just a couple of miles from Ilmington and about fifteen minutes from Stratford, their guest farm was a golden dream, a seductively sweet memory from a youthful visit, almost forgotten from thirty-five years of hard, steel city reality.

Still not sure if I should open the envelope, I picked it up, felt its perimeter, and looked again at the address label. Perhaps my grandparents had finally died and someone was sending word. Or worse, maybe they had indeed died, owing a lot of money to a nursing home, and now someone wanted to bleed me for the balance. There was a strong urge to toss the envelope out with the phony pizza and leave well enough alone.

"An ocean separates us, no one would come over to capture my '71 Buick to settle back indebtedness of an earlier generation," I mused.

Surrendering, I picked up the special delivery packet and slid a stained fingernail along the seal. In the cardboard carrier was a plain white envelope with the same attorney's name as was affixed to the cardboard carrier. My name was written boldly in cursive on the face of the envelope, with the flair of a confident legal assistant. Opening the envelope I pulled out a one-page letter. It read:

"Dear Mr. Bradbury:

If you are not already aware, I regret to inform you that your grandmother, Mrs. Caroll Hope Briscoe, has passed away and was recently interred. Our office was unable to locate a next of kin at the time of your grandmother's death, and we have since become aware of your mother's own demise through information gained from the Bethlehem, Pennsylvania county clerk office. Your address was provided to us by officials in that office.

Not able to contact a relative, the decisions surrounding final arrangements for your grandmother were made by a friend of hers here in Stratford, England. She was buried next to your grandfather in the historic Ilmington Church Cemetery, as was her wish.

Her personal effects at the nursing home have been stored and will be kept until we have a decision from you as to how to handle their disposal. There are, as you may realize, other personal possessions in her home, near Ilmington.

With her passing, there are a number of legal issues to be resolved which will require your kind participation. The single most immediate need is one concerning her home in Ilmington. I will soon file the necessary documents relating to her death and will forward those to you. At some point, you will want to contact the tax office in Stratford to record a current correspondence address in the United States for tax bills, etcetera, to be delivered, as I am sure you would not want her property to fall into delinquency.

We have in our office her check book which one of her friends delivered to us, keys to the property, as well as deeds to the croft. Please contact us as soon as possible to provide instruction in dealing with the matter. Until then, we will remain,

Faithfully yours,

John Hall, Attorney
28 March 1995."

I placed the letter on the opened envelope and leaned back, once again, on my mother's sofa. The brown corduroy felt soft on my calloused hands which I had spread out along the length of the cushions in both directions. There, sitting on the sofa next to me, was a wayward pepperoni, which I tossed to the waste basket. In its place was a small dab of tomato sauce, proof that even on this mid-life birthday I was still much a kid. I didn't even bother to wipe off the imitation red-colored splotch. All the talk in the letter about my mother and grandparents made me think about relatives, something I did not have, had not had for some time. It also made me think of the one relative I loved dearly but had never met, my father.

I pulled on jeans, tee-shirt, a light jacket, sneakers and headed out the door into the damp Pennsylvania air. Once I was in the Buick, the car took me (almost automatically)

across the river and into town. I drove by buildings and restaurants I knew all too well. The wet streets reflected the dark morning clouds as I drove down to the municipal park, pulling the car alongside the grassy area which was brownish-green from the cold but disappearing winter.

My feet slipped slightly on the damp ground as I made my way to a monument in the central area of the park. Once there, I knelt down beside the monolithic granite marker to locate the name, 1st Lt. William N. Bradbury. In seconds, I found the inscription honoring my father, a man I had never known. I ran my large, rough hands along the letters hoping, once again, to feel closer to my father who had disappeared in the last months of World War II.

I had seen him only in a few photos my mother had saved. The photos, along with his Medal of Honor, Distinguished Flying Cross, and the Purple Heart were kept in my top dresser drawer. These, along with a small envelope containing a few snapshots from my mother's childhood, are all the mementos I have of my parents. I loved my mother dearly, of course, but I cherish the photos of my father greatly; his medals have always signified a sense of courage and success, something he had, but which had eluded me for most of my life. He was a hero, a fighting hero, not at all like his common steel worker son.

He was able to come home twice during the War. The last time was in November 1945, an opportunity to conceive me and marry my mother; I've never been sure in what order that happened. My father helped fly a B-29 Super Fortress. His plane, Pride of the Yankees, was destroyed on its seventeenth mission near Saipan. One of the last photos taken of my father and his crew was of all the guys lined up beneath the fuselage in leather bomber jackets. Above them were four propellers, three of them shot to pieces. I suppose the props were replaced and they flew off, never to return. They must have been extraordinarily brave.

Somehow the monument, which my mother had often brought me to see as a youngster, gave me the feeling that 1st Lt. William Bradbury was, or had been, a real person. His remains were never found since the plane was shot down in the Pacific Ocean. But here, with his name chiseled in the public marker, I felt proud, a winner, which was a good feeling since mostly I felt a loser. No college, no marriage or children, and a half dozen jobs in the steel business. Forty-nine years to the day and not much to speak of in terms of what my father had accomplished by his young age of twenty-five. My hand swiped again across the slick stone-cold memories and I turned back toward the piece-of-crap Buick; my eyes watery from a swell of emotions which intermingled with the fine spring mist hanging in the air.

I drove through town and back across the Lehigh River. Several times, even recently, I had thought about just driving off the bridge, right into the icy water. I wasn't convinced I would die, so I never risked the possibility. Had I plunged into the river, the obituary would have been just a small news item — probably a single paragraph — on a back page. Alas, I am not a hero, I wouldn't be even in death. Flying past the drugged-like morning glories clinging helplessly to the rusty pole, I keyed the lock and zipped back inside to the chocolate colored sofa, the metal door slamming behind me. Once again, with the letter in hand I read about the need to "provide instruction in dealing with the matter." I wondered what was owed on the property if anything. How much money was in the checking account? Did I owe others money that would eat up anything left by my grandparents? Was this going to be just another big headache in a life already too consumed with headaches? All the answers awaited me in Stratford, England.

I remembered my grandparent's farm, or "croft" as the English say, fondly from a single visit in 1962. My mother had sent me to England the summer of my sixteenth birthday, to spend time with her parents and to give her a much needed break from dealing with a fatherless teenager. But mainly, she hoped the visit would help reestablish a long-broken relationship with her parents. That summer was perhaps one of the happiest times in my life. Actually, at first I dreaded going as I had never met my grandparents and I would be away from my sophomore year friends for three months. I feared that my grandfather would be some Nicholas Nickleby, ready to beat me with a stick each night before bedtime. I did not anticipate being a familial ambassador cum peacemaker.

The farm, called Hope's Croft for my grandmother, Hope, turned out to be a really nifty place. After the War they had bought the sixty-four acre plot strictly as a working farm. Because they needed extra money at times when the vegetable production or sheep market failed to produce enough income, they boarded guests. By the middle nineteen-fifties and with the growth of tourism, the croft became a bed and breakfast establishment almost exclusively. Grandmother Hope often told me during the summer I visited, that grandfather was a far better host than farmer, anyway. And so he was.

I remember he had two particular sheep, Larry and Lambkin, who he claimed were deaf. Guests would sit in white wrought-iron furniture out on the lawn and look amused when grandfather would say, "Those two out there, they're deaf as a rail!" Grandfather would stand at the fence bordered in Cowslip flowers and Ox-eye-Daisies, and yell at the top of his lungs, "Heeere Larry, heeere Lambkin, come to Pahpee, come to Pahpee." (Pahpee and Nanna were nicknames my grandparents used for each other, strangely enough though, since those affectionate names are normally taken up by grandchildren, which they never really experienced, other than my one visit.) The two sheep stared at my grandfather like he was from Northern Ireland. They didn't move a hoof. After a few seconds of his bantering, and after the sheep went back to snipping away at the lush meadow grass, he would turn to the baffled quests and proclaim,

"See they are indeed deaf!"

The guests were always amused. Some vacationers, those staying for a few days, would often walk out to the fence strung with thousands of white petaled-yellow centered daisies and long-stemmed Cowslip — while my grandfather was off doing some task — and speak softly to the sheep, hoping they might actually come forth proving grandfather wrong in his deaf assumption. Occasionally, Larry or Lambkin responded and the guests would correct grandfather politely at dinner.

As I recall, my Pahpee thoroughly enjoyed entertaining the people who stayed at Hope's Croft. He was a sweet man and it was unfortunate that my only time with him was the summer of 1962. Just from that one summer I know I would have enjoyed getting to know him better, but it was not to be. My mother's parents refused to travel across the Atlantic and I was never able to visit other than my one stay. They really never had anything to do with my mother after she left Stratford during the war. She had told me on several occasions that she jumped at the opportunity leave England because she was afraid of what the Germans might do. Once, when trying to figure out why her parents were so resentful, I thought perhaps my grandparents had assumed she left because she had become pregnant. That couldn't have been true, as the dates did not add up to that possibility, unless she had become pregnant several years before my birth. And if that happened, I was never informed…no brother, no sister.

Anyway, my grandparents weren't much on writing, neither was I, so we never kept in touch, even in the last years of their lives. Pahpee had been in a nursing home for a number of years before he died and I assumed that the B&B had closed down and that Nanna had given up the business, perhaps sold it. Because of the many years of estrangement, my mother and I figured we were not to be included in their will. We were wrong, or at least one of us was.

Outwardly, it didn't seem like my mother cared much for her parents or England. Maybe over the years she just gave up. I never really saw any desire from her to mend the relationship, other than my visit. During my stay on the farm neither grandparent talked much about my mother or father.

According to my mother, she and my father met in London in September 1941, not too long after Britain declared war on Germany. He was twenty years old and stationed at a British air base for training British soldiers. They met at Regent's Park following an outdoor music presentation in an amphitheater to entertain service men. She wasn't in the show, she just served refreshments to the soldiers, American and British alike, as part of a group of volunteers that came to London several times a month. She once told me, that one night after the entertainment had concluded, my father asked her if she wanted to go out to a pub, she agreed, and their relationship began. For many years, my mother had kept withered rose petals from a flower he had picked one night at Regent's Park.

The black and white photos of my father showed off his short-cropped hair, thoughtful dark eyes, and tanned skin. My mother often mentioned his six foot height, a measurement I topped by two additional inches. She also said I looked just like my father. His US Army-Air Force photo confirmed that fact. His enlistment papers recorded his weight at one hundred-eighty pounds, almost exactly what I had weighed all my adult life. No doubt he was firm from work outs and rigorous military training. The hand full of photos I have of my father made him look like a peaceful man, kind and understanding, with a courageous heart. There's no doubt we looked the same, but I certainly didn't feel a hero.

After my folks met in '41, he talked her into coming back

to the States while he was on a short leave, which she did. Even though she lived the rest of her life in Pennsylvania, she always was, in many ways, a typical English woman. She loved baked tomatoes for breakfast and took tea most afternoons. She had brunette hair, permed every few months, green eyes, and thin skin. She had a soft white face and thin lips. Mother kept her English accent until the day she died. During my teenage years, my friends, upon meeting Mother for the first time, would say, "Uh, Nathan said you're English, are you?"

"Of course, and what brings you to that bloody conclusion?"

My friends just laughed. So did she. So did I. Then my friends and I would go off and repeat the phase over and over, just exactly as she did with the same heavy English accent,

"Of course, and what brings you to that bloody conclusion?" Over and over.

Shortly after they came to the United States, Father was off flying missions in the South Pacific and there Mother was in Pennsylvania. She was far away from the battles of World War II, but also thousands of miles away from the rolling green English pastures of the North Cotswold landscape dotted with white splotches of sheep that she had enjoyed as a youth. No doubt she was lonely, but Mother told me a number of times how she felt much more safe in America than in the British country side during the war. In Bethlehem, we lived in a very small apartment, just above the garage at my paternal grandparents' home. Mother worked in an office in one of the steel plants from the month she arrived until she retired in 1985. Cancer claimed her life five years later.

Back during World War II, virtually all the women and children in America were left behind to understand the clashes through daily newspaper headlines, radio reports, movie reels and the occasional letters which were quickly opened and read, then hurriedly taken next door for friends and neighbors to review, with everyone in tears of happiness that their loved ones were still alive. When a letter was received that began, "We regret to inform you…," tears were also shed. Mother received *that* letter near the end of the War. Mother and Father barely knew each other before his life ended, but then that was the case with many young couples during this period, even couples where both individuals were Americans.

After my father died and following the end of the War, it would have seemed logical for us to return to Stratford, but we didn't. I never got an explanation. My father's parents in Pennsylvania helped my mother financially and with many of the other needs that come with raising a small child alone, which was far more than her own parents in England did. Her parents didn't even try to communicate with her after she left Stratford. As she told me, most of her letters to England went unanswered. I suppose it was difficult for them to understand how their only daughter could be so infatuated with an American boy, that she would leave home, even during a war. It was never discussed with me, but I suppose that my English grandparents were not too happy about their new fatherless American grandson. In the end, since I was a naturalized American citizen, it seemed we should stay in the United States. This was possible for both of us because I was a citizen by birth and she had been married to an American soldier. And that's the way things remained, with both of us in Pennsylvania.

My mother never remarried after my father's death. Neither set of grandparents had any other children, other than my mother and father. My American paternal grandparents died before I was thirty. No aunts, no uncles, no cousins. No hits, no runs, lots of errors! For the last few years I had been absolutely alone. And so now it seemed, via the letter announcing my grandmother's death, that Hope's Croft had been tossed in my lap to "liquidate." Perhaps, if there was some money to be made from selling the place, I could use the funds to buy a replacement for the Buick and, with greater luck, a small house?

"Wouldn't that be something, my first house before age fifty?" I muttered.

I folded the letter back neatly in the white envelope and took it to the only bedroom in my apartment. From under the double bed I pulled out an old suitcase, dusted off a network of spider webs, and examined it for durability. The bag looked strong enough to make a short trip to England and so I continued by cleaning the dark leather with a damp rag. Opening the suit case, and to my surprise, I discovered some fairly nice dishes my mother had left me. I had protectively placed them away in the luggage some time ago. The dishes had not been used since she had died and so I carried them to the small, white kitchen sink to be washed for later use. I placed them neatly beside the three dirty glasses and headed back to the bedroom to find travel clothes and toiletries.

After a quick lunch at a neighborhood diner, I picked up a morning paper and found a pay phone to arrange a flight to England. Luckily, a travel agent was able to locate a New York to London consolidator ticket which had been reserved by a group of students. It was available because one student was not able to travel. (I had to purchase a ticket from Philadelphia to New York to make the connection.) The flight was scheduled for late one evening the following week, which would make my arrival into one of London's airports early in the morning. I spent several days packing and repacking a few items and reading over and over again the letter from lawyer John Hall. Since my travel was caused by the recent death of a loved one I was able to get an emergency thirty-day passport at the county immigration office, in just a few days. The countless sick days I had accumulated over the years at the plant were available to me because of the death of a family member.

For one of the few times in my life I was really excited, excited about the possibility of actually having some money, even a little. My self-imposed isolation and the lack of anything fulfilling in life were temporarily set aside for the trip. Honestly, the death of my grandmother was not an emotional issue for me at all; as I said, I hadn't seen her in many years and we seldom communicated. Interestingly, it was strange that this event should happen to me on the downhill side, and slide, of life. I could hardly sleep all week, in fact, it was like being a youth of sixteen, all over again.

C H A P T E R   T W O

The British Airline 747 landed at Heathrow shortly before seven in the morning, the sixth of April. I was drowsy from the overnight flight and stiff from sitting in the same position for almost ten hours, an hour flight to New York and an eight and-one-half hour flight across the Atlantic. The group of friendly college students had been seated all around me from the New York leg of the journey, which kept things lively. They were from a small liberal arts college in the Blue Ridge Mountains and were also headed to Stratford where they were to complete a month long theatre course. The kids were excited about their plans to see Shakespeare's productions produced in his own home town.   For many of them, this was their first trip out of the country. For me it was the second, almost thirty-five years after my summer at Ilmington, but since it had been so long ago it really seemed like my first time to travel abroad, too.

The flight attendants were friendly and the food was good, a vast improvement from my nightly cooking in the microwave. The flight crew spoke English with a typical British accent, something I might have developed had we moved back to England after my father failed to return from the War. The British Airline stewards and stewardesses enjoyed bantering with all the passengers aboard the plane and were pretty good at picking out our various home states by listening to our regional accents. Of course, the drama students around me had skewed the process as about half of them attempted a fake British cockney. Others executed various accents which no doubt had come from characterizations in plays in which they had appeared. The group was clever and funny making the long trip enjoyable for me, but irritating to some around us.

I'm not much of a traveler, so the various steps to obtain my luggage, clear customs, and find ground transportation were really confusing, even though everything was in my own language. It seemed easier to just follow the group of students, which I did. Their leader, a theatre professor, seemed to have the process all worked out. Fill out the white card, present passport to officials, follow the non-declared line to baggage claim, and then out to the ground transportation lobby. The kind teacher sensed my feeling of confusion and welcomed me to follow along. The students told their instructor that I, too, was going to Stratford, so he insisted I travel along on their hired coach, which saved me almost forty dollars. After claiming my single bag, which fit right in with some of the bizarre luggage the students carried, we all stepped outside to the bus waiting area and watched for a big brown and yellow tour bus. Shortly, it came along and a couple of boys helped pitch the bags aggressively into the luggage compartment. Mine went in last, however the young men treated it more gently than their own, although there was no reason to do so.

The students adopted me and were fascinated by my story of Hope's Croft. Of course, they all wanted to come see the farm during their educational stay. I invited them to come out but warned them the old house probably hadn't been lived in for some time. It was that cordial chit-chat that people make when they have good intentions but don't usually follow through.

The English country side, up the M1 Highway, was a wake-up reminder from my youth. The rolling hills just turning emerald green, thatch roofs on old stone barns, herds of black-faced sheep waiting to be shaved of their thick, white winter wool coat, and, of course, the chaos of driving on the left side of the road. At every town along the way the big yellow and brown bus zipped through the roundabout. The British system of several highways and roads meeting at one point, where drivers turn left and circle round and round until the road they seek comes up on the left, could cause panic for non-experienced drivers. Actually, the roundabout system seems to get people "processed" through intersections much more quickly than the traditional method of traffic lights in the United States. I had forgotten about round-a-bouts, even though I had experienced them on a bicycle many times during the magical summer of '62.

Away from London the traffic became less and less heavy,

except at each town when we approached the roundabout, where traffic kept moving, but ever so slowly. First, Bushey then Watford, Hemel Hempstead, and Aylesbury. After about two hours we circled about Banbury and then were just a few miles away from Stratford. As we neared Stratford there was a real feeling of expectation among the students. They became quieter and looked out the windows soaking-in every image we passed: neatly groomed plots of land divided by stone fences, wild flowers and bulbs just beginning to bloom and little streams crossed by quaint rock bridges. The students, no doubt, felt a special bond to this, their destination, the hollow ground upon which their poet master sauntered and danced so many years before. It was special for each of us, though for very different reasons, because in the summer of 1962, I never saw a Shakespeare play performed in Stratford. I had never even seen one performed in Pennsylvania for that matter.

The big bus passed a long series of bed and breakfast establishments which lined both sides of the road, each proclaiming No Vacancies. Closer to the center of town, we crossed a long rock bridge with a sign announcing "River Avon" and finally pulled up to the center of town facing a giant steeple-looking clock, which I did not recall seeing during my adolescent journey. The bus rolled to a stop, the students cheered and a kindly old lady rushed up to the door of our coach.

"Yonah College?" she asked the bus driver to which he nodded assent.

The teacher jumped off followed by thirty-seven exuberant students almost in a frenzy to see plays, sight-see, study Shakespeare, and…most urgently, sit in a pub. I stepped off last and was handed my suitcase by the bus driver who was now alone, unloading everyone's luggage as they focused on the town center, home of William Shakespeare. I thanked the teacher and several of the students who had spoken most often with me on the flight and reassured them we would get together again in the coming days. The tourist representative directed me to 800 Rother Street, the offices of John Hall, Attorney. The office was just two blocks away, down from a quaint shopping area thick with tourists. I walked up to the Tudor office which had a charming frontage.

A series of unique window panes, each made from antique glass and molded in a circular pattern about eight inches across, traversed either side of the entry door. The same kind of round, thick glass appeared in many of the store fronts I passed on Rother Street.

The sturdy walnut colored office door, which looked to be hundreds of years old, was fitted with heavy black metal hinges and door knob. To the right of the entrance a clever name plate spelled out "John Hall, Legal Counselor" in a series of colorful ceramic tiles painted along with ivy and wild flowers. I went right in to Mr. Hall's office.

The office waiting area was only about twelve feet square and the ceiling was of rough hewn timbers, the same dark color and texture as the front door. The walls, covered in white stucco, and the hardwood flooring must have surely been old even when William Shakespeare stood nearby to discuss legal documents for property and plays, from some other lawyer. In what seemed to be an eternity, but certainly fine with me as I had seldom seen any building with so much character in my life, a young man of about thirty walked into the room.

"May I assist you?"

"Well, yes, I am Nathan Bradbury."

"Bradbury?" the young man repeated.

"Yes, I received a letter about my grandparents' place…" I said, pulling out the letter from an inside pocket of my leather jacket and handing it to the well-groomed gentleman.

"Oh, yes. My goodness, I did not realize you were coming, so sorry. I'm John Hall. I wrote you this letter, and my goodness you have come so soon, with such grand surprise."

I felt as if I had intruded on Mr. Hall and was somewhat uneasy because I suppose I was expecting him to be older.

"If I am interrupting you I can come back later. I guess I should have let you know I was on my way to Stratford. I uh, I don't own a pho…"

"Oh no, no, no, no, no. It is perfectly fine. I'm just glad I was here. You certainly traveled a long distance, you have."

"Yes, of course, I didn't think, I really am sorry," I stammered apologetically.

"Well, come in my office and let us get on with it. Tea?"

"Uh, yes, with sugar and lemon if you have some, please."

"Of course."

"And I prefer a lot of ice."

"Ice?" The man responded inquisitively as if I had just insulted him.

"Yes, ice, you know iced tea?"

"I'm afraid what I would be serving you would be hot tea. We drink our tea hot here in England in the afternoon."

"Oh, OK, yes, my mother...yes, hot tea it is, then," I conceded, reclining in one of his expensive looking leather chairs, finally remembering my mother's own tea habits.

Mr. Hall prepared the tea in a little kitchenette at the back of his comfortable office. He served me "hot" tea from an antique wooden tray and I helped myself to the sugar and lemon. His pin-striped trousers and matching vest were perfectly pressed and fitted to his thin, short body. He was a real gentleman. We sat at a small table in one corner of the room which contained an ash tray, a box of cookie looking things, and an antique pen and ink well. After delivering the tray, the attorney found a file from a drawer in a wood filing cabinet and sat next to me at the table.

"How is the tea?"

"Hot!" I proclaimed.

"Well, so it is. And the taste?"

"Actually, very nice."

Mr. Hall picked up the basket containing the cookie-like things.

"Scone?"

"Uh, I'm not sure...uh...what is a scone?" I replied ignorantly; my mother never made or mentioned scones.

With all the properness of an English schoolmarm, Mr. Hall gently informed me about scones and that these particular scones were raisin cinnamon. The gentleman made the cookies sound like a wonderful treat. I took a small bite. The velvety, sweet biscuit dissolved in my mouth like an ultra-soft sugar cookie, and I suddenly remembered scones, or at least their taste, from that summer.

"These are great…scones!"

"Now, Mr. Bradbury, may I call you Nathan?"

"Why, yes, of course."

"Nathan, as I said in my correspondence to you, I was sorry that your grandmother had died recently, February 28, I believe. Her friends took care of all the funeral and burial arrangements. I am really so sorry."

"Mr. Hall…"

"Please Nathan, John, just John is fine."

"John, I have not seen my grandmother since 1962. Since that time we seldom wrote each other. We were never really close at all. In fact I last saw her here in England when I stayed with her as a young boy. My father died in World War II, and my mother passed away several years ago."

"I see. Yes, we had difficulty attempting to locate her through letters found in your grandmother's home, and finally obtained your address from authorities in Bethlehem, Pennsylvania."

"Well, anyway, there are no other living relatives. There's just me."

"Nathan, let's take a look at what is on the table here. Your grandmother's home has no mortgage against it. It is free and clear and the taxes have been paid for the current year. The friend who took care of the funeral arrangements has kept bills paid from your grandmother's checking account, apparently for some time. The check book is here, also, and has a rather extraordinary amount of funds in it."

"How much?"

"Well, if the ledger matches the statement it appears to have a balance of about one hundred, twenty-five thousand pounds." Hall's small handlebar mustache seemed to curl up as he flashed me a quick smile.

"How much is that in American dollars?"

"Well, almost two hundred thousand dollars!"

I sat silently at Mr. Hall's little antique table. I picked up the check book and stared at the bottom line and then softly dropped the book to my lap. My right thumb massaged a lone age spot on my left hand, located between my left thumb and pointing finger. I looked back up at the youthful Mr. Hall, who still had a slight smile on his face knowing I was surprised by the news.

"I am really surprised by this. I had no idea she had any money at all."

"Nathan, your grandparents were very successful in running their bed and breakfast. You know it is located not too terribly far from town."

"Yes as a sixteen year old, when I stayed with them, I rode a bike into town... a number of times." I paused and thought pensively about the destination. "With luck, I might even be able to find my way there again."

"Well, with this kind of money you won't have to ride a bike to Hope's Croft. In fact, why don't I take you out there." With a quick snap, John Hall was on his feet.

"Now?"

"Shall we go?"

With that, Mr. Hall and I left the quaint office on Rother Street and headed toward Ilmington in his little red Fiat Spider convertible. He drove slowly, letting me see all the things I remembered as a youth: Holy Trinity Church, the peaceful walking trail beside the River Avon, and white swans everywhere. We crossed the Avon, passed the row of bed and breakfast houses, and headed southeast toward Ilmington. The two lane road was just as I remembered, curvy with many rock homes built centuries ago and thousands of flowers ready to burst into every imaginable color. We went across the Avon several times again before our ten minute trip ended in the Cotswold and down a rather long driveway near the door step of Hope's Croft.

John switched off the Fiat and jumped out of the convertible sports car like a kid. I sat in the left front passenger seat and stared at the three story brick home, holding back sudden tears of happiness. Funny, it was, for the second time in just a few days I had been on the verge of sobbing, something I had not done in many decades. How strange, this steel worker from Pennsylvania sitting in front of a magnificent old English home. What a far cry from my small apartment and unhappy morning glories. I climbed out of John's car and stood looking at the house. The farm house was faced in orange colored stones, slightly larger than typical bricks, and of varying shades and textures, just as I remembered, and had twin chimneys one on either end of the house. The roof, like so many others in England, was covered with gray tiles and still seemed sturdy from this distance.

We walked down a little path bordered on the left side by

a wood fence and to a gate needing repair. At the gate, a stone sidewalk of some fifty feet in length ended at the front stoop. Triangular Georgian stone work surrounded the entrance which beckoned all who approached to come inside. The door was vastly different from my metal clad door back in Bethlehem which frequently closed off all communication with others. Above this door was a half circle leaded glass window encased by the stone work. There were three sets of windows, a set on each of three floors facing the front yard. Even in this early spring time, tiny vines were creeping up the exterior of Hope's Croft orange stone walls like strange, green spider webs.

To the right, and slightly behind the farm house was a long stable, maybe seventy-five feet in length, made entirely from rounded, beige colored, rough stones and trimmed with shuttered openings carpentered from rough hewn lumber. Dark green English ivy grew all around the barn. The building was my secret retreat in the summer of '62, a place to hide and make new discoveries. The barn, as I remembered, was a lot older than the house.

"I recall that the barn and the house are from two different periods of time?"

"The house was built in seventeen-eighty-nine. The barn was built in seventeen-twenty, or at least we know it was there during that year according to the plat. It was perhaps built before that time."

Even though the house had not been occupied in years, it appeared to be in great shape, certainly good enough to sell and make a profit. John handed me the keys.

The keys were the large skeleton type, oversized by American standards and secured on a brass ring about three inches in diameter. I slid the largest key into the black metal key hole and turned. The door had to be pushed slightly and then gave way to my pressure, opening with a creaky sound. To our amazement, the house looked like someone had gone off on a vacation and was only delayed, somewhat, in their return. Furniture still in place, knickknacks on built-in stone and wood shelves to the left in the study and a sturdy wooden stairway straight ahead. The dining room to the right was set with china as if dinner would be served promptly at seven. It occurred to me, standing there by the dining room, that perhaps my own grandmother had set the table, years earlier, waiting for evening boarders. Most likely she was taken to a hospital and then a nursing home and the table was simply left ready for guests who never came.

Dust covered everything, floors, furniture, and door knobs. I asked John if I might look around and he laughed.

"What, at your own home? Of course!"

The first thing I had to see was a bedroom upstairs on the third floor. I walked steadily up three flights of stairs to a bedroom on the far right, the bedroom I had slept in during my visit. I pushed open the thick paneled door, affixed with the name *Foxglove*, and there was everything: same bed, same bureau, same window. The windows on the top floor were about half-as-tall as the windows on the first two levels and looked out to the lush green valley of the Cotswold. In a few weeks the hillsides would be covered in deep purple phlox, a memory that came back to me as I knelt down by the antique window panes, each containing the same circular pattern as those at Mr. Hall's office and frequently found all over the village of Stratford.

I headed across the hall, past a bathroom, to another larger third floor guest room. This guest room was appointed completely with Victorian furniture and included an en-suite bath, unlike my little room which only had a sink. My bathing was done in the hall bath which was also used as an extra bath for guests. After a quick look, I headed back down to the second floor. The four bedrooms on the second floor were appointed in attractive antique period furniture. Each bedroom on the second floor had a private bath. The rooms were in neat order and seemed only to be waiting a good cleaning and a guest.

Coming back to the first floor I could hear John's footsteps in the back part of the house near the kitchen. From memory, I made my way through a hallway beside the stairs, past a small den and to the enormous kitchen which seemed every bit as large as I recalled, which is unusual because things often seem to be much smaller when returning after years of absence, particularly places from one's youth.

John was standing by the sink, arms folded, looking at the various and sundry kitchen utensils, pots, and pans hanging above the large island in the middle of the room.

"You could feed an army with all these kitchen wares!" the attorney observed.

"Yes, we did, or my grandparents did. This is so unreal. I can't tell you how many meals I helped my grandparents prepare for guests when I was here. And there were cook books.

Dozens of them somewhere."

With that I began opening cabinet doors looking for the books. Behind each door was a multitude of kitchen cookery; bowls, cookie sheets, dishes, pitchers, china, silver ware. Everything one would need to put on the most elaborate feasts for friends and guests.

"Where were they?" Finally, I opened a pantry door near the back of the kitchen and discovered the "cooking library." Shelves and shelves of cook books from not only the United Kingdom, but all over the world. I pulled one off the shelf and opened the cover. Inside the inscription read:

Hope,
What a wonderful time we had staying with you and your husband. Your croft is a gentle place where meals, flowers and friendships mingle into a single experience. Please accept this, one of our favorite cookbooks from India, as a gesture of our friendship.

Namastay.

Dr. R. V. Kumar and Binka Reddy

June 1978

Bombay, India

"Namastay? What does Namastay mean?"

John, who was feeling the texture of a hammered copper pan which he had pulled down from the overhead rack, replied, "What?"

"Do you know any Indian? What does Namastay mean? Seems like…"

"I'm afraid I can't help you there, Nathan. Perhaps someone from one of the Indian restaurants near the Avon could assist you with your Namastay."

With that I set the book back on the shelf, in the correct alphabetical order just between *Icelandic Seafood Recipes* and *Iowa: Meals from our Heartland* and took one last contemplative look at the shelves of cookbooks. The collection had grown considerably since I first saw it as a youth. There must have been three or four hundred books, all from different cultures, different countries. My guess is that many of them contained similar inscriptions as the Indian book, no doubt gifts from guests who had stayed at Hope's Croft over a forty year period and found my grandparents to be very special friends and great cooks. Opposite the books in the pantry were dozens of electrical kitchen appliances, shelves full of them.

Closing the pantry door, I asked John what he thought the property was worth.

"You know, it is a splendid place. With the acreage —over sixty in total— the river frontage and potential as a business investment for overflow guests from Stratford, not to mention its historical significance, I could successfully market the property in less than ninety days for, oh, three-hundred maybe four-hundred-thousand pounds."

"That's…"

"Well over half-a-million US dollars," John replied in a British voice that sounded as if he were announcing a recent lottery prize in a lowered, controlled adult voice.

I rubbed my eyes with my hands and shook my head to the good fortune that I had just inherited. "What would I do with half-a-million dollars?" I thought deeply.

John looked at his watch and announced it was time to head back to Stratford. I begged to stay longer to which he agreed, and then said he would return to the office for a short meeting. He offered to locate a plat of the land and would come back to the farm in a few hours, before dark.

"The electricity has apparently been shut-off for some time so you wouldn't want to stay past dark. I'll return before sunset." John extended his hand to shake mine good-bye and departed with the salutation, "Congratulations, Chap!"

The afternoon sun broke through the kitchen window illuminating the room in golden rays which gave the copper pans hanging over the island a rich look, even in their dusty state. The light warmed the kitchen and I had the strange impulse to fix a meal in this house that was temporarily mine. A house in which I had returned to remember the summer of my sixteenth year. With no food, no electricity, and a fading afternoon I decided instead to walk around outside of the B&B.

I unlocked the back door in the kitchen and stepped out unto a stone porch that led down to a beautiful rock veranda laid out in a giant semicircle. The patio once enclosed half-a-dozen tables at which guests could enjoy the evening sunset

or early morning tea. A rock wall about three feet high surrounded the patio which had several openings so visitors
could meander into the flower and herb garden. Even without a caretaker, flowers were just beginning to sprout in the
beds which completely surrounded the veranda. The tiny
flowers were competing with a carpet of weeds throughout
the area. I walked out the opening on the right side and
looked up to see the barn, one of my favorite places in the
summer of 1962.

I smiled and continued walking around to the front of the
house to the view across the Cotswold. I looked across a pas-
ture which was secured by the fence. As I could make out,
down a hillside was the small River Stour which joined the
Avon just down the road. My God, the memories were coming back to me like I was watching an old video tape movie in
slow motion, rewind position. I jumped the wood fence,
which almost gave way under my weight and trotted through
the glen to the banks of the Stour. There, just as I had remembered, was a tree. A tree that had once had a rope tied to an
outermost branch, providing me countless Geronimo jumps
into the cool summer water. The rope was long gone, but not
the memories. I crouched down beside the river and felt the
water, much too cold for a jump today.

I stood, surveyed the area once more, and headed back to
the house. Going in the front door, I turned to the left into the
study which was lined with bookshelves on just about every
wall. Comfortable antique furniture was scattered throughout
the room, placed so one could read, work puzzles, or play
cards. I made my way around the study examining every lit-

tle knickknack, English doily, and piece of furniture.

"How would I ever take any of this stuff back to Pennsylvania?" I pondered. On the far side of the room, opposite the door was a rock fireplace bordered by shelves containing novels and historical books from throughout the world. Covered with dust, the books included just about every well known work, as well as many obscure titles. It was truly a unique library for guests to enjoy.

As I turned and continued around the study, a closet door revealed games, jigsaw puzzles, birding equipment, and a few quilts. Guests always felt free to rummage through the closet for table games, binoculars, whatever they wanted, or needed, to make their visit like home. Hope saw to that!

Finally, before making my way completely around the room, there was a narrow shelf that spanned floor to ceiling. On these two-foot wide shelves were guest books, all in chronological order. The book on the far left of the top shelf was marked 1948, and on the binding of the last book, located on a lower shelf and to the right, was written, 1990. Apparently, my grandmother had received guests until 1990. I pulled out the most recent guest register and opened to the page in which the final entry was written. The date September 20, 1990, was entered in the far left column. In the larger middle section titled "COMMENTS," the following appeared:

Mrs. Briscoe,

Thank you for a delightful week at Hope's Croft. We are sorry you felt ill last evening. We hope you are able to see a doctor Monday morning and that you will feel better again soon. Pace and I know running a B & B like Hope's Croft can be difficult, especially by yourself. Tell Mr. Briscoe we were thinking of him. We'll stop off at the nursing home in Stratford and leave some shortbread with the nurse. We remember you saying that raspberry flavor was his favorite. Wish us luck on our trip to Greece. Mykinos is a wonderful place for a wedding trip, but not nearly as homey as Hope's Croft!

Take Care,
Patricia & Pace McDonald IV
Edinburgh, Scotland

I slid the most recent guest book back in the shelf and perused the colorful collection of registers kept by my grandparents. There were five shelves in all, each year documented in a single book. Several years were actually scrap books containing photographs of guests staying during the year, as well as recipes served them. Hope would take photographs of many of the guests, particularly those she really liked. That way, Pahpee and she could enjoy looking back at all the friends they had made over the years. Because of the number of visitors, the photos helped remind them of who-was-who. My finger traced books from one of the upper shelves:

"1952, 1958, '60, yes, 1962!"

With curiosity, I pulled the 1962 guest book off the shelf and opened it. I flipped through the months until I came to June and then sat down in one of the dust covered leather chairs opposite the blackened fireplace. The sun was getting lower on the horizon but there was still an hour or two of daylight left and plenty of it was spilling into the room from two large windows, lighting the pages that recorded the guests from my summer visit.

In writing that appeared obviously immature, and seemingly out of place from all the other hand writing, a note had been entered. The date, June 8th, had been scribbled in the left column. The immature writing, that of a male teenage guest, left me with goose bumps:

My first day at Nanna's and Pahpees.
The trip was really long but I'm finally
here. I have my own upstairs bedroom,
named Foxglove, with a neat window and
wow, what a kitchen! It is a lot different
than our apartment. I don't think there
are any guys here my age, but maby I'll
meet someone neat. Who knows? Pahpee
Showed me a bike which will be fun.
He says I might can ride it to Stratford.
There also is a river he says, with a
rope swing. Hope I meet some friends!

Nathan, age 16

Pennslyvania

It was startling to realize I had flown all the way to England to rediscover the old house and of all things to find the note entered in the guest book, over thirty years ago, in my own hand writing. Extraordinary, it was.

The next page was dated June 9th. The two guests who had signed were the first I had met at Hope's Croft. They were twin sisters from Italy, and quite a pair of matched bookends. They had frizzy black hair, olive skin, and oversized hefty bodies. A photograph in the guest book, opposite their handwritten entry, was an accurate picture, not only in looks but in personality as well of the two women. They were standing next to the stove in the kitchen, wearing large brown paper grocery bags as tall chef hats, each decorated with different types and colors of uncooked pasta in a variety of shapes. Italian phrases had also been written on the bags, which looked more like strange top hats than chef hats since the edges had been rolled up to make them fit snugly. Matched toothy grins stared at the camera while each of the women held an assortment of kitchen utensils. Between the sisters, squashed among two oversized sets of very well-developed motherly breasts was a sixteen year old youth, smiling gleefully, wearing his specially made chef hat too, and acting silly with a tea strainer and kitchen tong.

Sitting in the dusty but now warming leather chair in Hope's Croft study, in the quiet and peaceful solitude of the present vacancy, I stared at the youthful, happy youngster in the black and white photo. He seemed to enjoy all the attention heaped upon him by the two gregarious women. Where did the carefree feeling go in that boy? Why did the young face in the photograph seem so different and far removed, so alien from its older, current clone? Gently, I pulled the faded photograph off the page, to stare even more closely at a smooth young face gone so long ago from an aging, lonely old man.

CHAPTER THREE

Briscoe's and Hathan,

Well, we have certainly enjoyed this week! What wonderful food and company, and it went by much too fast! Thanks ever so much for letting us help in the kitchen, again. We're taking our homemade hats back to Italy. We will also take the new British recipes back to The Venetti Cafe in Florence.... Won't that surprise the Italian customers and international tourists? We really enjoyed helping Pahpee feed the animals and the "unplanned" swim with Hathan in the river. We'll never forgive you Hathan, you naughty boy! By the way Hathan, if you ever visit us in Florence we have a niece your age who you must meet. She's "molto bella!" (Very beautiful!)

Love Always and Grazie,

Maria and Marcie Venetti

A swell of emotion came over me as I read the entry from the Venetti sisters. The two women were like smothering mothers who caressed and cared for me continuously. Actually, Pahpee explained several times that it was my job to care for the guests, not the other way around, but these two never allowed that. From the first minute I met them, they seemed like long lost foreign aunts who couldn't be close enough to me. It was scary at first and then I came to enjoy it. The last day or two of their five day visit I came to depend upon it.

Each morning one or the other, Maria or Marcie, would rise early, make cappuccino and bring a cup to my room just as the sun began peeking over the Cotswold, spilling golden light into my small third floor window. The sun made an interesting design on the wall over my bed as it shone through the antique glass window. The single round pane of thicker glass caused the light rays to focus more sharply in a series of three or four circles, the center of which looked as if the light was coming through a giant magnifying glass. The lighted circular design made its way slowly down the wall as the sun rose and I always knew if it had made its way halfway down the wall to the bed, I was late for helping with breakfast. If I saw the pattern on my quilt upon waking, it was too late, period, and I would be welcomed by a sink full of dishes.

That never happened the first week as the Venetti sisters made sure I was up with a cup of their own homemade cappuccino, normally mocha. This was achieved by making strong coffee, adding a flavor from the huge spice cabinet in the pantry, and then boiling milk in a small, specially pressurized kettle they took along with them on their travels. The hot chocolaty-coffee, sugar added, was a warm welcome to cool English mornings. The cappuccino arrived each morning just as the sunlit design appeared near the ceiling. Maria, the more serious twin, brought me a cup on their first morning and awakened me with her Italian-laced English, sitting beside me on the single bed.

"*Buon giorno*, dearest little Nathan, it is time to awake for a wonderful summer morning!"

"What, uh, OK. Am I late for helping with breakfast?"

I asked, startled that the large lady I had only met the day before was comfortably seated next to me as I slept.

"No, my sweets, you are not late at all. How was your night of sleep? Dressed in warm dreams of fantasies, I hope?"

An embarrassed smile crossed my face.

"No, I, I, I, don't think so. Just plain sleep. But good sleep."

"Nathan, you must get up soon and come down stairs to tell Marcie and me about your life in America. Your grandparents have never really told us much about you in all our many visits."

"Sure. OK. I'll be right down."

"You are such a handsome young man," Maria said, while gently pinching my cheek softly between two fingers topped with bright red Italian fingernail polish.

When Maria left, I jumped out of bed, grabbed a pair of jeans and sweat shirt, and looked down the hall before racing to the bathroom for a quick shower. Once finished, I zipped down stairs where my grandfather and the Venetti twins were seated at the dining room table. Nanna was in the kitchen just about to bring out the dishes of traditional English breakfast. After a quick greeting of "good morning," I headed to the kitchen to help, but was instead urged by Marcie to sit at the table, which I did, but only with Pahpee's nod of approval.

"Nathan, *buon giorno*. Hope you rested well?" Marcie quizzed and smiled.

"Yes, of course."

"Nanna said she would be right out with breakfast, please do tell us about your home in Pennsylvania. Pahpee said you have just arrived."

"Well, it is a steel town called Bethlehem. My mom works as a secretary. My dad is…"

I stopped and looked at my grandfather who completed the sentence for me.

"Nathan's father was killed in World War II. "

"I am sorry, Nathan, I didn't know," Maria added gently.

"Here is the fine English breakfast of roasted tomatoes, scrambled eggs, link sausage, bacon, and toast, toast, toast!" Nanna announced entering the dining room and carrying a giant tray.

Placing the tray on the center of the massive wood table covered by a hand-stitched white antique table cloth, Nanna added, "Not at all Italian, but wonderful nonetheless, splendid and traditionally English!" Nanna lifted a wire toast holder off the tray and placed it between the twins who each took a slice, and added a "thankful" *Grazie*, before moving it toward Pahpee. He took a slice and then handed it to me. What a neat outfit it was, a chrome wire toast holder. It could hold up to eight slices of toast, standing at attention, just like stoic British soldiers guarding Buckingham Palace. It seemed appropriate for England and a far more proper way to display toast than our way back in Pennsylvania of just piling it on a saucer. I took a slice and passed the holder to Nanna, who added *Grazie*, in her British accent, which evoked a chuckle from the twins, Pahpee, and me.

Next came a plate of roasted tomato halves. I did not like tomatoes, even on a burger or sandwich, and certainly not warm and mushy. And to eat one for breakfast? Well, you know, sometimes you feel compelled to join in, particularly when you have been "joined in" by your neighbor. The tomatoes came to me by way of Pahpee and I just held the plate, looking at the strange, withered dollops of red fruit. They stared back. I started to pass the plate on to Nanna, all the remaining tomatoes intact, when one of the twins barked up.

"Oh Nathan, these are just speciale! Ooooh! Let me help you," Marcie gushed, taking a spoon off her own setting and reaching across the table to move a warm, oozing red love fruit to my plate with a plop and a broad Italian smile. I glared at the tomato first and then raised my eyes to the twins who both seemed to be frozen in happiness, like delightful Italian faces off an American tomato paste can.

I eked out a weak, *Grazie*, and passed the plate to Nanna.

"Now let's see, you don't fancy baked tomatoes in America, do you?" Nanna asked and continuing, "You really must give them a try, Nathan. They are most extraordinary."

Around came bacon, which I did like, still soaking in a lot of fat. I took two slices and waited for the eggs, which looked pretty normal. With plates loaded, we began to eat.

"The eggs are great, Nanna!" I observed, hoping no one noticed that I was eating my way *around* the bright red tomato in the center of the plate.

"And the tomatoes are…," Marcie added.

"Perfect!" Maria completed.

"Nanna is a pretty good chef," Pahpee praised.

Marcie carefully spread homemade fig preserves on her toast and crunched a large bite, and then quizzed, "Nathan, have you found Ilmington to be satisfactory?"

"Satisfactory?"

"You know, do you like England?"

"Yes, of course, what I've seen so far. We saw neat houses on the train from London. Pahpee told me about each little town we went through. He met me at the airport."

"Did you talk to Larry and Lambkin?" Maria asked.

"I tried, but they're deaf," I responded.

The group snickered at my naivete.

"Aren't they?"

"Of course." "Why yes!" "Indeed." "Deaf as a rail," they added.

I finished off the eggs and toast, bacon, too. I kind of liked the bacon still floppy and we didn't have bacon too often back home. Finally, everything had disappeared from my plate except the tomato. I started to cover the plate with my napkin and politely take the plate to the kitchen. But Marcie caught me.

"Nathan, my *bambino*, you did not eat your tomato? It is the best part of breakfast. Even Italians appreciate the morning tomato. Won't you even try it?"

I gulped, "Well, you know, we just don't eat too many tomatoes in America for breakfast. We don't want to create a tomato *shortage* around the world for British and, of course, the Italians," the group laughed at my slight humor.

"Go ahead, Nathan, just one bite," Maria urged, followed by silence and stares.

"It is so tasty," Marcie added, seducing me with a smile, as if there might be some magical potion in the little red thing.

"Nathan, when in Rome, do as the Romans!" Pahpee whispered in a quiet command.

"Nathan, I worked so hard!" Nanna's lips puckered as if she might burst into tears that I would dare reject any part of her traditional English breakfast.

I could see great expectations on their faces as I glanced around, looking at my circle of breakfast mates.

My adolescent mind begged for cultural familiarity; Rice Krispees, Post Toastees, even oatmeal. But no, it was now obvious that I was going to put the warm, red mushy slime in my mouth. In my mouth of all places. I picked up the fork and knife and began slowly cutting the tomato in half. The others sat quietly as if I were preparing to dive off a giant cliff, watching my every move, urging me on with anticipative smiles to see if I would be victorious in meeting the British breakfast custom head-on…or if it would choke me to death. I chose the smaller of the two chunks and looked up at Marcie who was now holding a salt shaker toward me. Still silence.

"Salt, oh, of course salt," I *thought* to myself and continuing only in my mind, "I couldn't possibly get that down my throat without some salt to cut the taste."

I took the salt shaker from Marcie, almost in slow motion, and shook more than enough salt on the tomato, thinking it might even kill the taste. Everyone seemed to be leaning even closer toward me, their faces becoming more and more intent on my placing half of the tomato in my mouth. I pushed the fork in and began lifting the small red fruit toward my head hoping that something, anything would happen to divert the attention so sharply focused on me by these unfamiliar relatives and friends. The fork came closer and closer to my mouth, tomato perched on end, smiles broadening. Marcie and Maria mumbled Italian phrases of encouragement — in soft almost chant-like voices — Nanna and Pahpee glared at me with supportive smiles, then finally, I opened up and the tomato went in — and down — like an oyster being swallowed by a non-sea food lover being coerced by intoxicated friends. It was gone, so quickly, that I virtually had not tasted it at all.

The room cheered and applauded. The twins spouted Italian congratulatories. My grandparents clapped wildly. As the commotion subsided, I added in an unsure Italian accent,

"Grazie, grazie, grazie!"

The English breakfast was over.

I helped clear the table and was asked by Nanna if I would wash the morning dishes. She showed me exactly what to do, carefully removing the dishes to the wash room, no dish washer, it was all done by hand. We filled the sinks, one with soapy water, the other with clear water. I carefully washed all the dishes, pots and pans, rinsed them, dried them all off, and placed them neatly on the large island in the middle of the kitchen. Almost an hour later Nanna, who had visited with the Venetti sisters in the study, examined my work, thanked me and discharged me of further duties for the morning.

Pahpee was outside feeding Larry and Lambkin and the other menagerie of animals that he tended which gave the B&B an authentic English country look. He asked me to help, which I did. After a while, the Venetti twins came outside and asked if I wanted to go down to the River Stour.

"Of course!"

"Why don't you go put on a swim suit? Did you bring one?" Marcie inquired.

"Yes."

"In Italy your response would be, *'Si'*."

"Si. Si. Si-Si." I responded like a silly teenager.

I rushed inside, leaving Marcie to talk with Pahpee.

In minutes I flew back downstairs, out the door, to my new friends who knew the path to the river quite well from previous visits. Each wore a colorful dress, Italian sandals, and a big floppy straw hat to shield them from the sun. They also wore expensive looking sun glasses. Each carried a straw-woven hand bag filled with books, note paper, a small blanket, snacks, and other items for an afternoon of rest and relaxation by the river.

The walk to the Stour was less than ten minutes, and followed a path through purple phlox. The Stour was crystal clear and flowed past Hope's Croft on its way to merge with the River Avon. Willow and oak trees grew all along its banks. One particularly large oak had a long rope attached to a sturdy branch which stretched out across the river. The river was about twenty feet across and about six feet deep at the center.

The ladies stretched out their blankets and urged me to make a big jump into the river.

"We have jumped many times before, Nathan," Maria responded.

"Actually, I have jumped many times. Maria has only jumped a time or two. But today, since it is earlier in the summer than when we normally visit, we'll leave all the jumping to you, Nathan," Marcie explained.

"Well, here goes!" With that, I climbed up to a platform nailed to the oak tree, about five feet off the ground, grabbed the rope, and swung out. I went almost all the way across the little River Stour, and back, before letting go of the rope and falling about ten feet to the surface with a splash."

"Wee-ah! My gosh! It's freezing! Whew!" I screamed upon resurfacing.

I swam to the grassy bank and jumped out of the water, shaking drops of cold water all around my friends.

"Nathan, stop, you're getting us wet. You silly *pesce*!" Maria chided.

"Maria, don't call the boy a *fish*, he's just a silly *Americano*," Marcie added.

"Boy, is it cold! I've got to get back in!" I shouted, goose bumps covering my legs and arms. I climbed up to the platform again and jumped a second time, making a few drops of cold water splash too close to the Italian sisters.

"Nathan. You must stop. We are going to be sorry we

brought you down here. Just make small splashes when you let go, and let go more toward the other side of the river, *per favore*."

"Sure," I agreed and continued jumping.

At last, I crawled out of the water and sat down near Maria and Marcie and promised not to shake on them. They threw me a towel and told me to dry off. After doing so, I stretched out the towel on a carpet of thick green grass and gazed up through the trees. Marcie handed me a fruit drink, and got her and Maria a glass of wine from a bottle resting in one of the two straw bags. It was a light red wine and looked very sweet. They drank the wine from glasses Nanna had given them earlier. Maria pulled out a loaf of sweet Oatmeal bread and shared a piece with me, before passing it to her sister.

"Nathan, how is your juice?"

"Great!"

"Oatmeal bread?"

"Terrific," with a mouth full.

"The wine is good, *Ravello Rosato*, from our neighbors in Salerno, Italy," Marcie added.

"You are very nice ladies," I announced.

"Thank you, Nathan. We think a lot of you, too. Even though we are new friends, your grandparents have been dear friends of ours for many years. We enjoy the annual summer break from our restaurant in Florence and love letting someone else cook for a few days," Maria explained, taking a long sip of wine.

"Is your restaurant big?"

"Well, Nathan, no. But big is not always important. Our restaurant is owned by our parents and before that, by our grandfather. It has been in the same location, near the Duomo, for over seventy years. And actually, there has been a restaurant in that same location since before 1900, only owned by someone else before our grandparents operated it. No, it's not big, but it is perhaps the *best* place to eat in all of Florence," Marcie said with a self-assured chuckle.

"What is the Duomo?"

"The Duomo is in the center of Florence, it is the central cathedral, with a giant cupola top, visible from most all points in the city. It was built over five hundred years ago by Brunelleschi."

"Is it neat?" I asked, which was followed by a pause from Marcie.

"Well, it's, it's better than neat."

"I'd like to see it some day."

"You must come visit us, then," Maria added, who sipped further on her wine glass.

I ate another sizable chunk of Oatmeal bread, and washed it down with the juice.

"Is wine good?" I asked.

"Yes, *buono*!"

"What's *buono*?"

"Good!"

"Can I try some?"

With that, Marcie smiled and poured the last remaining portion of the blush wine into my cup. I had never tasted alcohol before. Mother simply didn't drink. I sipped the wine and was surprised at how good it was, sweet and mellow. Certainly better than the early morning tomatoes.

"*Buono*!" Drinking from my cup, wiping a pinkish stain from my upper lip, and taking yet another bite of bread.

I could see that the ladies were relaxed. They laid back on their blankets and looked up through the sun which danced through the leaves like a thousand little needles of summer light. Maria, sat back up on her elbow, and looked right at me.

"Nathan, I talked earlier with Nanna. We talked about you. I asked her some questions because in all the years we have stayed at Hope's Croft, she never told us about a grandson. There aren't any pictures of you around her home. That seemed strange so I talked to her."

"Yes."

"Well, she said there were some problems. She said that your mother had left back during the War. We have known that for some time. She has mentioned, in the past, that she had a daughter in America, but she never discussed a son-in-law, or you. And, honestly, all that seemed strange to me. Do your mother and Nanna write each other?"

"No, I don't think so. At least I never see any letters," I added, growing reluctant to discuss the topic much further.

"Nathan, my sweets, do you know what the problem is?"

"No. Not really."

"I asked your grandmother why she didn't have a photo of you out on a table, or somewhere, that you were such a handsome young man. She just said there were many hard feelings between your mother and her, that a photo didn't seem appropriate," Maria shared.

"I really don't know what the problem is, or was. I just know there is a problem. They are mad at each other, always have been. I can't stand it, though. And now that I'm here, this place seems so neat. Why wouldn't they want to like each other?"

"Nathan, it must go back to when she left England and married your father. It must have something to do with that. I am so sorry you are caught in the middle of this. You are such a fine young man. I hope it all works out. I know it will," Maria ended.

I jumped up and ran for the platform, grabbed the rope, pushed off toward the cool waters of the Stour. I swung back and forth a few times, gaining momentum with each passing by pushing off the platform with my feet. After three or four swings, I let go heading toward the tree and splashed a ton of water on the sisters with my fall. They screamed.

"Nathan, I'm going to get…" Maria jumped up.

Marcie just sat, astonished that she was wet, and smiling nonetheless. When I crawled out of the water, Maria chased me around the grassy area, trying to grab my swim suit, arms, anything she could hold onto. I'm sure half my rear-end was shinning skyward after one of her tight grips of my swimsuit. In short order, she came back around to the blanket area, under the tree, and got out another bottle of wine. I sat down, a little breathless, too, and watched as the matron of Florentine table manners uncorked a second bottle of *Ravello Rosato*. She poured us *all* a drink.

"You are really fun. Both of you," I observed.

"Well mostly Maria, she's the wild one. I'm the motherly

one," Marcie contributed.

"Well, I can't believe I'm having this much fun with two…"

"Yes," Maria replied with a snap, not waiting for me to complete the sentence; adjectives, descriptions, etc.

"Two…friends!" Glad I had rethought whatever it was that might have come out of my mouth.

We sat for a awhile longer and finally, the three glasses of wine began to make me a little dizzy. I was feeling really relaxed and happy, ready to forget the problems of my family. Once the bottle was finished, we decided to head back to Hope's Croft. I stood up, folded my towel neatly and handed it to Maria who thought I was handing her my hand for steadiness. Unfortunately, I was not prepared for the weight of Maria Venetti, and she slipped backward as she rose to her feet. Completely off balance, Maria tumbled backward several feet further until, with tremendous surprise to us all, landed in the River Stour…with a giant splash. Marcie and I ran to her rescue, but you must realize that trying to help a two-hundred-twenty-five pound woman out of a slow moving river with slippery banks is not easy. On our third attempt, I fell completely back in the river, almost on top of her. We both laughed hysterically, and eventually stopped trying to get out. Laughing, we floated out to the middle, each enjoying the cool water and break form the seriousness of the earlier conversation. Maria's dress began floating in the water until it was up around her midsection, just below her giant breasts.

"Are you all right?" Marcie questioned from the bank, holding her own dress up high with petite fingers, so as to not drag it in the water around her chubby ankles. _"Perche ride?"_ she asked.

"I'm _laughing_ dear sister because this is so much fun. I've never swam half-naked with a handsome American young man!"

Marcie gasped, "Maria come out of there, now, _capisce_!"

"No."

Maria was obviously having more fun than she had had in a long time, or so it seemed.

She laughed and said to me, _"Quanti anni ha?"_

"Maria, no, no, he is a , boy, only a boy! _Il bambino_!"

Marcie ran to the tree. Maria's dressed was floating up to her neck, about to float completely off her body. All she had to do was pull it over her head and it was gone. I wondered if my grandparents could see, or hear, all that was happening down on the River Stour.

Maria was facing away from the tree, across the river, and holding on to my arms to stay afloat. I was in front of her, facing the tree, my feet just touching the bottom of the river. I looked up and could not believe what was about to happen. Marcie was on the platform holding the rope. I stared over Maria's shoulder, astonished to see the other half of the twin Italian sisters jump off the perch, and swing toward us. At first, I prepared myself for a rather large splash but it did not come. She had swung over us, continuing on, and was now clearly over the other half of the river. At the pinnacle of her swing, Maria now, for the first time, saw her sister way up in the air, coming back toward us. What a sight it was! As she passed over, I ducked, Maria ducked, but Marcie didn't

release. Back toward the tree she went, pushing off the platform with her feet. We surfaced, only to see her pass by yet
again, both of us fearful of what would happen if she let go,
which she didn't, at least not yet. With each passing, which
became slower and slower, we dodged Marcie. Finally, like a
engine out of steam, she came to an absolute stand still over
our heads, miraculously still holding tightly to the rope. Her
grip, no doubt, had come from years of kneading bread
dough. There she hung, suspended in air, directly above us,
screaming Italian phrases which I did not understand but pre-
sumed to be appropriate for the situation.

"*Scusa, penso che questo sia il mio posto!*" She screamed, looking straight down at us and releasing the rope, her arms
pointed toward the heavens, toes toward the water.

With a gigantic splash, Marcie's plunge tossed us around
like beach balls, a most inappropriate scene for a proper
English countryside.

After all three of us resurfaced from the Italian tidal wave
and when the water calmed somewhat, a real surprise awaited us. The force of the skyward jump had completely stripped
Marcie of her dress like someone, "skinning a cat." But that
wasn't all. The impact of Marcie's ten foot drop from the rope
and her sisters' quick plunge to avoid being hit also dislodged
Maria's dress which had been hovering around her neck.
There I was, swimming with two Italian women, shrouded
only in laughter and undergarments. A lot of undergarments.

After we had had enough, I agreed to push the ladies out
of the river from behind, which was a humbling experience
for us all. The dresses were gone forever down the Stour, and

curious, I asked Marcie what she had yelled just before she let go the rope. The big lady laughed and translated in English for me,

"Excuse me, but I believe you are in my *seat*!"

As we passed through the gate and into the front yard of Hope's Croft the ladies, sans their dresses and dripping wet, nodded at Pahpee who stared silently at the three of us. Larry and Lambkin? They stared, too.

Upon returning from the swim, Nanna asked me to clean up and come to the kitchen to help her in making more Oatmeal bread. Along with all the fun with the Venetti sisters, the bread had made the afternoon an even sweeter experience. Unfortunately, we had consumed the last of the loaves bank side. This was my first opportunity to cook alongside my grandmother Hope. She showed me around the kitchen, explaining the bowls and utensils we would need, and where to find the ingredients in the large walk-in pantry. First, we set the oversized oven to 350 degrees. Then I got the following items out of the pantry from a list Nanna had given me:

> 1 cup Oatmeal
> 1/2 cup whole wheat flour
> 3/4 cup brown sugar
> 1 Tablespoon salt
> 1 Tablespoon cinnamon (optional)

And from the refrigerator:

> 2 Tablespoons butter

Nanna got out a big mixer and had me combine the above

ingredients in the glass mixing bowl. Then we heated two and one-half cups water, until boiling, and poured it into the same bowl and mixed for about a minute. After mixing, my grandmother gave me a large glass thermometer which I placed into the batter. She told me to watch the temperature carefully, and to tell her when it had fallen just below 130 degrees. Once the temperature had fallen below 130 degrees, we added the following:

> 4 cups of bread flour
> 2 packages of active, dry yeast

She told me that occasionally she had to add a little more flour when the humidity caused the dough to be too sticky to handle, sometimes even over a cup. At this point we placed the mixture into a large wood kneading bowl. She showed me how to knead the dough; pushing, stretching and folding, for about eight minutes. The dough was then placed into a lightly greased bowl, covered, and kept warm until it had doubled in size. After the dough had doubled, we divided the mixture in half, shaped into neat loaves, and placed each in a regular size bread pan which had been lightly greased. We "painted" each loaf with fresh milk, using what looked like a small paint brush, and then sprinkled each loaf with rolled oats. Once again, we covered the loaves and let them rise until doubled in size. She pointed out that letting the bread get too big could cause it to collapse. Both pans were then put into the oven and baked about thirty-five minutes.

The aroma of the kitchen that afternoon was something I

had never experienced in my entire life back home. The odor of freshly baked bread made with oatmeal is a special experience. It was one thing to eat the delightful bread with the Venetti sisters, quite another to know how to actually make it. I felt like Nanna was letting me in on a big secret, known only to us. Fact is, later I discovered she'd shared every recipe she had with anyone who wanted them. And in return, many of those who came to stay at Hopes' Croft, even for a short visit, would leave a recipe they thought grandmother Hope and her guests would enjoy.

After the loaves cooled, we placed one in a plastic bag and then into a pastry cabinet located on one wall of the kitchen. The remaining loaf was placed on a round, green marble cutting board beside a bread knife, covered by a clear glass cake cover, and positioned on the dining room table for spontaneous enjoyment. The bread was best when sliced about 15 minutes after coming out of the oven. Once finished, I cleaned all the utensils, bowls, and counter tops and replaced everything where it belonged. My second kitchen task at Hope's Croft completed. And, from what I have since learned, Oatmeal bread was one of the trademarks of Hope's Croft Bed & Breakfast.

The Venetti twins each had a room to their own, both on the second floor. After they cleaned up, following the swim, the ladies took to bed for a while. After resting, and sobering up a bit, they came down stairs to visit and asked if they might take me to see Holy Trinity Church. I wasn't used to going to church, particularly on a Tuesday afternoon, so I listened quietly hoping that maybe the idea would fade.   However,

Pahpee agreed to let the ladies take the car to Stratford and so off we went. We drove by a long line of B&B's coming into town and crossed the bridge over the River Avon. We turned left and followed a series of small signs to Holy Trinity Church. Finally, out of curiosity, I asked why we would be going to church on a Tuesday afternoon. The ladies just laughed.

"Nathan, we are not going to church for a church service, we are going to see the tomb!" Maria parked the car near the giant old cathedral.

"What tomb?"

"Shakespeare's. William Shakespeare's, of course!" The two got out of the car, Marcie in front, Maria in back, and walked toward the ancient stone church surrounded by large tombstones. I jumped out of the car and looked up at the giant spire. There was never a church like this in Bethlehem.

I caught up with the two ladies and walked between them.

"You mean William Shakespeare is buried here? At this church?"

"Yes, Nathan, you didn't know that?

"No. Not at all. No one ever told me. Which marker is his, they're all so tall, like everyone was real important?"

"Well, he's not buried in the *yard*," Marcie offered. "No, not the Bard!"

"Where then?"

Together, they opened the door of the church and stared at me, responding in unison to my question, "Inside!"

Wide-eyed, I passed through the door and into Holy

Trinity Cathedral. The ceilings were so tall, so ornate. Lectures were being presented in small groups to visiting tourists. Maria and Marcie seemed to know just where to go. They headed to the front of the sanctuary, looking like they worked there. We passed rows of pews, an organ, and sculptures. Near the front of the church, they handed an older lady a few British pounds and we went right through an opening. Suddenly we were standing in front of a small roped-off area. The ladies looked down and said, "There."

Sure enough, there was William Shakespeare's name etched into the floor. Along side were the names of other members of his family. I couldn't believe it. In school, we had just read *Julius Caesar* only a month earlier and now, here he was, buried, right in front of me. Right there on the floor. In all my sixteen years I had no idea where Shakespeare was buried, or if anyone even knew where he was buried. I guess I assumed it was so long ago, he was just lost. Guess I was the one who was lost. We stood looking at the spot a few minutes longer and then walked around the inside of the cavernous sanctuary. It seemed the whole world was opening up for me at that instant, and two totally strange women were responsible. Even at sixteen, I could see what a gift was being shared with me. Shortly, we left, and made our way back through the eerie looking grave yard surrounding the cathedral, and walked to a large grassy area nearby.

The large, flat, well-groomed area was playing host to a kids' carnival. The carnival featured children from the town who were doing all kinds of acts: magic, scenes from Shakespeare's plays, juggling routines, dance, costume competitions, and yard games. The event was to raise money for the church and about two hundred people were milling about helping the cause and being entertained. A small group of youthful musicians playing the flute, mandolin, and violin performed music that made me think of Shakespeare's era. At a face painting booth, all three of us had our faces painted to look like various animals; Marcie was a walrus, Maria a tiger, and mine was painted to look like a monkey. Soon we headed back to Hope's Croft just in time for Nanna's wonderful supper.

When we got to the B&B, we snuck up to one of the outside front windows, one in the dinning room, and peered through the thick glass. We could see Pahpee placing silver ware around the plates and grandmother Hope bringing in glasses filled with water. The two looked up as we made funny faces through the window. When they saw us, they screamed and ran out of the dining room. We went inside to find them in the kitchen discussing the strange sight. Upon seeing us they were somewhat relieved. No wild animals, only some bazaar actors from Stratford.

We decided to leave the face paint on for supper and sat down to a wonderful meal of tender lamb with mint sauce, sweet carrots, and red-skinned new potatoes with fresh string beans. Dessert was a plate of lemon flavored scones. I helped clean the table, wash the dishes, and then headed to bed. Just before I drifted off to sleep, I heard Marcie whisper loudly in the stairwell to me, "Nathan, have you ever eaten stuffed tomatoes?"

"No," I answered back in the same loud whisper, not

wanting to know in anyway what she meant.

"You will, tomorrow! *Buon Sera*."

The next morning I awoke early and beat the Twins from Italy, to the kitchen. I helped Nanna with, yes again, the traditional English breakfast. The ladies came down and were surprised to see me. They prepared their cappuccino, making a cup for me, also, and we all stood in the kitchen helping Nanna with the last few details, loading the wire toast holder, and moving the bacon to the serving platter. We ate at a patio table on the stone veranda that morning, which Pahpee had preset for us. During breakfast, just about the time the roasted tomatoes came by me, Maria announced we would be making stuffed tomatoes for dinner.

"Oh, that would be marvelous!" Hope responded, adding, "A night off for the chef."

"*Si*, and it will all be done by Marcie, Nathan, and me," Maria explained.

"I hope you know how to make stuffed tomatoes, I sure don't," Nathan revealed.

"Certainly, it is the 'Oatmeal bread' of the Venetti Cafe."

I looked down at the tomato on my plate, placed there by me this time, and wondered if stuffed tomatoes were any better than plain baked tomatoes. After breakfast, the twins and I walked down the road to the center of Ilmington to get some things they needed for the evening meal. Once in town and after buying the small bag of supplies, we walked further down an alley-like path, to the old Ilmington Church. The church was ancient, and like the Holy Trinity Church, was surrounded by tall grave markers, only these seemed older.

The place kind of scared me so I suggested we head back, which we did.

I was instructed by the twins to meet in the kitchen promptly at four-thirty PM. I spent most of the afternoon cleaning out the horse stalls in the old barn, pulling a few weeds out of the wild flower garden, and playing with a big turtle that had crawled up to the veranda. I must have spent an hour trying to get him to emerge from behind his closed door to eat a variety of delights I thought he might enjoy. A dead spider, leaves from Yellow-Horned Poppies which covered most of the wild flower garden, and a piece of string covered with bacon grease. Nothing seem to suit the hard-shelled fellow. Each to his own.

Promptly at four-thirty, I washed my hands at an out door spigot near the barn and headed for the kitchen, I could hear the Venetti sisters inside, Italian music softly floating from one of the large windows. They greeted me with hugs as if I had been gone for weeks, though it had only been a few hours. The two were each wearing a giant hat, made from a large, brown paper grocery bag with the edge rolled up as a brim. Each bag was covered with different varieties of pasta, in different colors, glued to the paper bag. Elsewhere on the hats were Italian words printed in markers of various colors. Music of some romantic Italian love song played softly in the background from a small record player brought in from the study by Maria. Upon entering the back door, my own Italian paper bag hat, decorated with dried macaroni, green noodles, and bow-tie pasta, was placed on my head.

"Perche impiegate tanto tempo?" Maria asked, while taking

me into her arms and dancing me around the spacious kitchen to the lovely music.

"He's not *late*, my dear Maria, he's right on time," Marcie corrected.

"*Si, si, si!*" Maria responded, adding, "*Scusa, per favore.*"

The song ended and Maria kissed me gently on the fore head, which required her to stand on her tiptoes and me leaning down slightly, my hat almost falling off.

"Now we will make stuffed tomatoes," Marcie announced.

On the giant island the following ingredients had been assembled:

Eight large firm tomatoes, 4 to 5 inches wide
Salt, about 1 teaspoon
Olive oil, 2 Tablespoon
Two small onions
Five cloves of garlic
Three cups of Italian-seasoned croutons
Three Tablespoons of parsley
Two Tablespoons of capers
1/2 cup pitted black olives
Three Tablespoons of freshly grated Parmesan cheese
Two Tablespoons of finely chopped fresh basil leaves
Two cups of chopped, cooked spinach
Three cups graded mozzarella cheese

A bottle of red *Merlot* wine sat on the counter, it never

went into the recipe, but disappeared anyway by the time the dish was completed. I was instructed to chop the onions which I did. Marcie showed me how to use a garlic press to squeeze each of the five cloves of garlic, but only after they were peeled. I also chopped the black olives up into little pieces. While I was hacking away at these, Maria sliced 1/4 inch off the top of each of the eight tomatoes. Then, carefully, she cleaned out most of the insides of the firm tomatoes with a spoon, leaving about a 1/4 to 3/8 inch shell. It didn't bother me at all to see the red guts of the tomatoes go down the drain.

The onions, garlic, and black olives were placed in a cast iron skillet, along with two tablespoons of olive oil, and gently cooked until tender. Ooh, what a smell! Afterwards, these were combined with the graded mozzarella cheese, chopped spinach, chopped basil leaves, and Parmesan cheese. Marcie cut the capers into little pieces along with the parsley and placed those in the bowl as well, along with the dried bread crumbs. I was instructed to turn on the oven to 375 degrees, which I did obediently as the sisters sang in unison a verse from the current love song playing on the record player. The song was romantic, kind of sappy, but it fit the women, the recipe, and the smells emerging from Hope's Croft kitchen.

The inside of each tomato was brushed with olive oil and then lightly salted. The stuffing mixture seemed kind of dry so we added a little olive oil, but not too much. Finally, each of us began gently stuffing each tomato with the mixture, careful not to hurt the tomato. Once stuffed, the fruits were dusted with buttered bread crumbs, placed in a lightly greased glass pan and placed in the oven. We didn't talk much while

making the recipe; the music, foods, and odors seemed to provide most all the communication needed. We cleaned the
kitchen, the ladies drinking more wine and still singing. The
tomatoes would bake for about 30 minutes.

We wiped the counters, replaced left over spices in the
pantry, and the wonderful smell from the oven mingled with
the natural odors of Hope's Croft kitchen on that summer
afternoon. The basil, garlic, and olive oil permeated the air,
converting the olde English kitchen briefly into a classy
Italian sidewalk cafe.

There we stood in the clean kitchen, our giant brown
paper chef hats balanced on our heads, music fading in the
background, and a simple supper on the way. Before going
upstairs to clean up and change shirts, the ladies grabbed a
camera from a purse and coaxed Pahpee, who was out on the
veranda, to take our picture. Standing by the big stove, crazy
Italian hats on our heads, and each holding various kitchen
utensils, Pahpee snapped, the camera flashed.

"One more," Marcie encouraged Pahpee, but not before I
turned, grabbed two remaining, unneeded and uncut giant
tomatoes off the island, and stuck them under my tight, white
tee-shirt as pseudo breasts. The ladies smiled toward the
camera, unaware of what I had just done. All three sets of
breasts stood out plump and firm, Pahpee recording the
moment forever on film. Marcie and Maria, turning and finally seeing what I had done with the tomatoes, chased me
around the kitchen, the tomatoes bobbing up and down in my
tight shirt, and finally ending up on the floor. Squashed flat,
the red goo had splattered the side of the island, my shoes, just

about everything. Chased out of the kitchen and up the stairs, I got ready for supper.

Nanna set the table, took the tomatoes out of the oven and called us to the dining room. All I can say after eating this dish, *Pomodori Ripieno*, was that I never again disputed the wonderfulness of tomatoes. The meal was an epicurean delight accompanied by the same sweet music that had played earlier in the kitchen. After dinner, Nanna and Pahpee cleaned the kitchen, Maria went upstairs, and Marcie and I retired to the English study for a game of chess.

"The tomatoes were great! Pick a hand.?" I instructed.

"Lefty. Looks like I'll be black. Yes, Nathan, sometimes you just have to manipulate ingredients to make something extraordinary and exciting out of something you find objectionable. Wonderful isn't it?"

"No doubt," not really understanding the depth of her comment.

I moved a pawn and asked Marcie about her parents.

"They are in their sixties and still operate the Venetti Cafe. Maria and I do most of the work in the kitchen and sometimes greet customers. The place is always full, we must chase off the customers late at night or they would never leave. You would like it, we don't serve roasted tomatoes for breakfast. We don't even serve breakfast."

"Are they nice, your parents?"

"Oh, yes. Mama is like Marcie and I put together, well not that big, of course…" Maria moving her first piece.

I laughed a little, after all, she had made the funny remark.

"But her heart is wonderful and she knows everyone in Florence. Papa is strictly business. He is a good businessman, but not as fun as Mama."

I inched the pawn to another square.

"I didn't know my father, as you heard Pahpee say a few days ago. He died when I was a baby. He died in a plane crash. The plane was shot down in the War in the Pacific Ocean. My mother has a lot of medals that were given to her after the War. I wish I had known him. I miss having a father. I miss it a lot."

Ignoring the game, Marcie reached out to hold my hands in hers.

"Nathan, you are such a sweet young man. I wish things were better for you. I wish I could bring you a father. I wish somehow I could just bring him back for even a short time, so you could see him, know him. Hold him."

Staring into her deep, dark Italian eyes, my own began to water. I pushed the game out of the way, spilling the board and game pieces on the floor, before grabbing Marcie Venetti around the neck. I sobbed for my helplessness. Helplessness of missing my father, helplessness for not being able to understand why my mother and these two wonderful people, Nanna and Pahpee could not get along. I cried for quite a long time, quietly, my tears splattering the hard wood floor. Marcie's tears also flowed freely and we held each other for awhile.

"My sweet, precious *bambino*," She said tenderly, holding my head, stroking my hair. My sweet *bambino*."

Soon, it was time to go to sleep and hope for better understanding in the future. Together, we climbed the stairs finding all floors dark and quiet. The kind lady kissed me on the forehead as we stood on the second landing, my tall, brown paper chef hat fell to the floor.

"*Scusa,*" she said apologetically.

"Good night."

"*Buon sera.*"

I picked up the funny, brown paper hat and up the stairs I went.

The Venetti sisters stayed a few more nights and then left on the morning of their fifth day. I was given the task of bringing down their luggage, which consisted of two large trunks. Obviously, they did not handle the luggage themselves, instead relying on taxi drivers and porters. Carrying each of the trunks down the two flights of stairs from their rooms named, *Coneflower* and *Sabbatia*, I wondered how many more bottles of *Ravello Rosato* and *Merlot* were hidden away for their journey back to Florence, and hoped that their clever chef hats were not getting crushed.

The ladies skipped the traditional breakfast and ate a quick meal of bread, jam, and fruit, and then waited in the study for their car and driver to arrive from Stratford. The driver would take them to the train station where they would return to London for a few days, before a quick trip to France, to stay at a winery owned by friends, and then on to Northern Italy. The Venetti twins had friends everywhere.

I was sitting out on one of the trunks when Marcie stepped outside and settled next to me. She placed her arm around my shoulder.

"You are going to be just fine!"

"Thanks."

"There is an Italian saying, '*Il tempo sana ogni cosa.*' which means, 'Time heals everything.'"

"I believe you."

A dark maroon taxi from Stratford pulled up in front of Hope's Croft and I yelled for Maria. Marcie hugged my neck one last time, kissing me gently on the forehead. Maria, Nanna, and Pahpee came out and we hauled the luggage to the giant trunk of the car. I stood back and watched the two, thirty-five-year-old Italian women get into the taxi with the driver closing the doors behind them. Swiftly, the car backed up, pulled out of the driveway, and down the country road away from the B&B. I could barely see Marcie's soft hand with red finger nail polish in the window of the big car, gently waving us a warm…*buona sera*!

❊❊❊

The sun still blazing through the study windows, I turned a page in the 1962 guest book to see the entry of the next visitor at Hope's Croft, Christina Siljan, a "retired" model from Sweden.

CHAPTER FOUR

Hope's Croft,
  Thank you. Thank you very
much for a most memorable
weekend!
      Your friend,
      Christina Siljan
        Sweden

Memorable is a word I, too, would have used to describe three days with Christina Siljan. From the moment Nanna asked me to answer the front door of Hope's Croft on June14th, I knew this striking blonde woman from Sweden would be a lot different from the Venetti sisters. Siljan, (she preferred to be called by her last name), stood only an inch or two shorter than myself. Slightly less than six feet tall. Her hair, almost white, not white like an older persons white hair, but Swedish white, was shoulder length. In contrast, her skin was a light bronze, as if perpetually fed by the timeless rays of the Scandinavian sun, and yet somehow made tough by the cold North wind. Her body was lean and firm. Fingers, arms and legs all long, unnormally long. She could have easily been a Viking goddess worshiped by a herd of Thors.

Oh, Siljan why couldn't I have gently folded you into my adolescent suitcase in the final days of my visit in 1962, making you my life partner? Instead, I have lived almost fifty years, alone, only to dream of your image for my selfish satisfaction, a thousand times over. The image of your sleek body lying before me like captured spoils of war, to be licked and suckled like one does a wound, has never escaped my memory. Not a lifetime of laboring over burning hot metal, not living on continents separated by a vast sea, not even the passage of time has erased the seconds joined end-to-end that made up our few moments of togetherness at Hope's Croft.

Late in the afternoon on the 14th, a soft knock was heard on the thick front door. Just a small sliver of amber sun shown through the half-circle, leaded glass window above the door, which I had opened way too abruptly. My eyes focused on her midsection, slightly above actually, and then traveled to her face, which was hidden by large red-rimmed sunglasses and a droopy, wide-brimmed red hat that covered her hair. It looked as if she were wearing black leather boots, under the long, loosely fitting black dress. The dress displayed her braless breasts, exposing them only on the upper halves, but exposing them nonetheless. This new guest was not at all akin to the former twin sisters from Florence, that was for sure.

Siljan arrived as an overused outcast; a leftover from the

Swedish model scene of the 40's. Fifteen years earlier she was every bit as hot as the molten pig iron that glowed yellow-red in a Bethlehem steel furnace. She had been sought after, not only from Swedish dress designers, but international ones, as well. Her long slim body, almost freakishly long, graced the cover of every fashion magazine in the world. Soon after her arrival she had explained to me that the world knew her face, her body, her name, Siljan!"

"Hell-o, my name is Christina Siljan. I don't have a reservation, but I was wondering if you have any vacancies? It seems most all the B&B's in Stratford are full."

I never heard a word she said, my eyes still fixed on the breasts.

"Excuse me, are you all right? Did...did you hear me?"

"Uh, yes ma'am. Yes. I'll get my grandmother."

Leaving her standing in the doorway, without enough sense to invite her in, I headed back to the kitchen to get Hope, tripping first on a broom leaning on the staircase which I had just used to sweep the hallway.

My grandmother and I came back into the entry hall to find Siljan seated on a small chair beside the guest book table and the front door closed. The new guest from Sweden stood for us.

"Good afternoon," Nanna announced to the new unre-served guest.

"I was wondering if you might have space available for a few days. Seems like all the inns..."

"Are filled to capacity in Stratford," Nanna interrupted and continued, "yes, of course, we do have room for you, and as a bonus, no crowds, no rowdy pubs around the corner, and far fewer auto horns honking than you are likely to find on Rother Street this time of year. Just sign the guest book, and Nathan here will take your things to the second floor. You do have bags don't you?"

"Yes, they are outside with the driver, by the gate. Perhaps, Nathan could carry them for me?" Siljan responded, placing her long-fingered hand on top of my head and patting it like you would a puppy.

"Of course, be right back!" Feeling a little funny that a stranger, particularly someone as striking as this new guest was so comfortable touching me so quickly after just meeting me. After all, we were in Britain, where hugs and kisses stopped at the English Channel.

Outside, I got Siljan's two suitcases from the driver, and headed back toward the door. Seconds later, I heard the distinct sound of a British throat being cleared impatiently and turned to see a hairy hand outstretched from the navy blue blazer the driver was wearing. I set the bags down, walked back over to him and pulled out the only money in my pocket, a US one-dollar bill. I didn't look at the old man, but I did hear a very clear and distinct, "Gah-Blimie!" followed by a rather aggressive door slam. I didn't ask Nanna what the word meant, but later in the summer I did hear Pahpee say the "Gah" part several times when he was upset about things around the barn. I had never heard the word used back in Pennsylvania.

Once upstairs, second floor, in the *Evening Primrose* — a room just beneath my own room — I placed the larger of

Siljan's bags on a wooden suitcase stand and left the smaller one in the closet. The luggage was nice, but well-worn from years of travel. I was looking up at the ceiling, on the way out of the room, and ran right into Siljan coming through the door, knocking off her red straw hat and glasses.

"I'm sorry," I responded quickly, crouching down to pick them up, but pausing briefly to stare at the tight leather boots laced all the way up her leg, and disappearing out of sight beneath the black dress. I stood up, handed her the hat and glasses, trying to avoid looking at her breasts, and for the first time saw the white hair. It shocked me. Before, down stairs, she looked so sophisticated with the hat, glasses, and all. But now, the long white hair falling down both sides of her face and onto the coal black dress material, she seemed relaxed, friendly, and even flashed a slight smile. She touched the top of my head again, after taking the hat and glasses, but instead of a cordial pat, this time her hand fell down the back of my head tracing the outline of my hair and neck. The touch gave me goose bumps, but a different kind of goose bumps than the ones I had while swimming in the River Stour with Maria and Marcie. These goose bumps meant business. Did she?

I wasn't waiting around to find out. I apologized again and zipped out of her room and back down stairs to the kitchen, where Nanna was assessing the possible need of preparing an evening meal for us and the lone guest. You have to understand that in town, most B&B visitors received only breakfast, just like the name suggests. However, out in the English country side, guests often were fed an evening meal, as well. Sometimes, if a guest were going to town for theatre, they would have a car pick them up and then dine at one of the eclectic restaurants in Stratford. For the most part, though, once they had arrived at Hope's Croft they were there to stay. Usually, guests had "done" Stratford before they visited us, or it was the next stop on their travel plans. The B&B was a destination, not a rest stop.

"Did you get Ms. Siljan's things to her room?" Nanna asked.

"Yes, ma'am. She's there now. Will she eat with us?

"We'll need to ask her, Nathan, but I suppose she will. You know, we weren't expecting her, so I'll need you to take some fresh towels up. Why don't you ask her if she would like to join us for the evening meal, say around seven-thirty? The linens are in the closet by the washer, take her two towels, wash cloths, and a new bar almond soap. You might also ask her if she'd like to join us for a drink before dinner."

I fetched the towels and soap and headed for the stairs. I stood looking up the stairs and wondered what she was doing. Was she in the bathroom? Changing clothes? Trimming her toe nails? Orders were orders, so I climbed the long flight of stairs that matched the eleven foot ceiling which seemed endless. My hand fidgety, I knocked twice gently on the door, and then considered placing the items on the floor and running like hell.

Siljan opened the door.

"Yes, Nathan?"

"Here are some towels. Would..."

My voice cracked in typical teenage fashion.

"Would you like to eat with me? Us? I mean would you

be eating with my grandparents and me tonight? This evening? At seven-thirty?

"Nathan are you nervous about something?"

"Uh, no. No not all. Nope!" I paused and forfeited, "Well, yes, I was afraid I might drop all this stuff before I gave it to you. So here," handing her the items and dropping the soap, anyway. At least I was consistent. This time her bare feet greeted me, the boots were resting comfortably elsewhere. Her tanned legs, just as the boots had done, disappeared up in the darkness.

"Yes, Nathan I would enjoy having dinner with you, I am famished."

I handed her the soap.

"Thanks. *Dra mig baklanges*, bellboy!"

"What does that mean?"

"Well, literally, it means, 'You drag me backwards!' But, as it was used, it is a Swedish saying that, 'You are unbelievable, Bellboy!'"

"Oh, please don't. I am not really a bell boy. I'm just visiting my grandparents for the summer. I live in the United States. I'm not a real bell boy, at all. Not at all."

"Well, then, you can take this kronen back and show your friends some Swedish money, here."

She reached for her purse, hunted for a second, and then placed a blue and green Swedish bill in my sweaty hand, made so by the late June heat, and even more so by the temperature of the situation. Siljan gently closed my fingers around the bill and stared right at my eyes while holding my left hand firmly in both of hers. She captured my hand like an arm wrestler making the first offensive move, a move against a new opponent not familiar with the strength or weakness of the opposition. My heart raced like crazy, wanting to do anything but stand there and look into her eyes. You have to realize that it wasn't that I didn't want to look into her eyes, it's just that it made me terribly self-conscious, like she was sizing me up. Was she?

I gently pulled my hand back, thanking her for her generosity and telling her dinner would be served at seven-thirty, in the dining room. As I headed down the hall I remembered.

"Drinks in the study before dinner if you'd like?"

Sticking her head out the door and replying, "Of course!"

Soon, lying on top of my bed, with the door closed, I could hear the water running through the pipes in the walls of the *Evening Primrose* room. The water continued for some time, filling her tub. She was undressed now, taking a bath in a room just one floor down. The white haired lady from Sweden was naked, her long dark body stretched out in the white porcelain tub, the sweet smell of almond soap filling the air all around her. All I could think about was seeing her breasts, the black boots, her white hair, and my hand wrapped in hers; the feel of my warm wet sweat coating both our hands, while standing at her door. Suddenly, these images were interrupted, interrupted the way a man's erotic thoughts are quickly bounced back into reality by something he doesn't want to hear. In this case, by the silence of her bath water no longer flowing.

I sat on the edge of my bed thinking I, too, should probably clean up for dinner and for the current guest in Hope's

Croft. I got clean slacks, underwear, a button down shirt, dashed into the hall, and into the bathroom I sometimes had to share with guests. There, with door securely locked, I took off my clothes, and turned on the hot water faucet in the tub. I wondered if she was listening to the sound of the running bath water, *my* bath water. Did she even know it was my water?

Once the tub was full, I took a bar of soap and washed my body, causing the sweet smell of almond to fill the warm June air around me. Below, just a few feet away and separated only by wood flooring, was Siljan, making gentle sloshing sounds that were only slightly audible. Looking over the edge of my tub, at the floor, I wondered if she could hear mine?

Dressed in dark slacks, white buttoned down oxford shirt, and red tie I pulled on a thin navy blue, v-neck sweater. In the June evening, with the windows open, a light sweater was desirable.

I went to the study at seven o'clock sharp to find an empty room, a chilled bottle of wine, and three clean wine glasses sitting on a silver tray. *Three* glasses: Siljan, Nanna, and Pahpee! Nothing for the little boy from America, accept probably juice, later. The tray had been placed on the chess table, chess pieces neatly positioned below on a lower shelf. I sat in a leather chair and waited. Longer. A little longer. I wondered where she could be, did she fall asleep after her bath, stretched out across the bed? Was she in the kitchen helping Nanna? No, not likely for a stranger, not even an outgoing one. Was she to miss the "drinks" to which she had been invited? Finally, I saw the answer to my questions.

Through the front study window, I could see Siljan seated comfortably on a white wrought-iron bench in the front yard. She was holding a bunch of Ox-eyed daisies in one hand, and in the other, a wine glass! There had been four! It occurred to me then, that had the forth glass not been intended for me, I could always plead ignorance on my part to my grandparents. After all, surely Maria or Marcie had quietly let it slip that we had had a little too much vino on the banks of the Stour. They had returned without their clothes. And, well, this was Europe.

I picked up one of the three glasses supported by a dark, rose-colored stem, and poured me a glass of the deep red wine, then headed out the walnut colored front door. Siljan looked up at me on the stoop and smiled, I smiled back, and walked across the thick green grass to the outdoor furniture. She invited me to sit, to which I did.

"What an attractive sweater and tie, Nathan."

"Thanks, you look nice, too."

"You mentioned earlier that you were from the US, where do you live?

I told Siljan the usual stuff, a story I got used to telling by the end of the summer. She was attentive to my comments, touching me softly on the sleeve several times as I talked. She asked questions along the way, learning all about my past, and seeming genuinely interested, even laughing at some of my remarks and squeezing my arm even more tightly. I did hide my frustrations and fears about the family squabbles, though, to which I had confessed to Marcie a day earlier. This new guest was not a mother figure. Didn't want her to be.

Once we seemed to have covered my turf, it appeared as if she wanted to share some things about her past.

"Nathan, I told you earlier I was a model, I might as well..."

"Nathan, Ms. Siljan, were about ready for dinner, come join us," Pahpee announced with a booming voice from the stoop and destroying my attempt to hear the other side of the coin.

"Be right there!" I shouted back, holding out my noticeably drier hand to support Siljan's getting up from the bench.

"You are a real gentleman, Nathan!"

Going inside and closing the door behind us, Pahpee announced, "We mashed yet?"

Facing away from my grandfather and my eyes opened wide, I wondered if he thought we had gotten drunk?

"No, I don't think so," I responded carefully.

"Well are you read for a cupper?"

"What?" I asked, my eyes moving from full circle to a squint.

"Are you mashed, you know, are you ready for tea? Cupper tea?"

I smiled and looked at Siljan who was just as confused.

"Oh, I see, you both still have your wine. Well, bring it along to the table and we'll save the tea 'till afterwards. Come along." Siljan and I took our seats at the table, facing across from each other, Nanna and Pahpee on the ends. The table was set with white china and shinny brass silver wear with rosewood handles. A napkin was placed appropriately in a round brass napkin ring at each setting.

"Angels on Horseback?" Nanna offered.

I looked at the plate and gave a small chuckle, was she trying to spoil the mood I had been setting for the last thirty minutes, I thought to myself?

"You know, oysters, oysters wrapped in pig bacon, and grilled on the barbee," Nanna explained.

"Excellent," Pahpee observed, galloping several "Angels on Horseback" to his plate.

"Well, I suppose I'll have one, couldn't be any worse than..." Wanting to say "baked tomatoes" but fearing for my life.

"Oh, I'm sure they are delightful," Siljan added, carefully placing one on her plate, and then up to her mouth.

"Not bad, not bad at all," I observed, taking a bite.

Next, Nanna handed Siljan a plate of roasted young quail which had been wrapped in grape leaves and baked. Each of us placed one on our plates and continued by self-serving fresh, hot wheat bread spread with real butter, small creamed onions, and steamed asparagus.

"My mom doesn't serve food like this back home," I said, once again, thinking too late, or perhaps not at all. Mentioning my mother so casually at this point in my visit was still a mistake.

"Well, this is a special occasion, Nathan," Siljan, saving me from a dead end conversation, and continuing, "Mrs. Briscoe, what is the stuffing in the quail?"

"Apricot, walnuts, and clotted cheese."

"Clotted cheese?" I asked, putting the current chunk of quail back on my plate, hoping for an explanation that would not turn my stomach.

"I believe, in the States, that would be *cream* cheese," Siljan offered, coaxing, without further objection, the tasty piece of bird back to mouth.

"This is really good, Nanna!" I complemented, reaching for another whole bird.

After we had eaten everything Nanna had set on the table, Pahpee went to the kitchen and brought out individual Buttery Bread Puddings baked in hand-thrown pottery bowls.

Nanna explained how she took a big bowl of stale bread, mixed it with two cups of milk, added a cup of butter and heated the mixture gently.

"It's all in the slowness. You mustn't rush this dish," Hope Briscoe commanded.

"Then take two cups of chopped fruit, a little more milk if necessary, a teaspoon each of nutmeg and allspice, four or five hen eggs, and stir it like that American boy, Elvis, moves his hips," Nanna smiled. We laughed.

"You have to bake it, don't eat it raw, " Pahpee added.

"Oh, yes, bake at about 325 degrees for two hours and then sprinkle brown sugar and a little more butter on top the last little while in the oven."

"It's the national dessert of England, approved by the House of Commons," Pahpee proclaimed. We finished off all four bowls of Buttery Bread Pudding and sent for several more. The four of us ate the entire batch made by Nanna earlier in the day. The unexpected guest was now happily satisfied and looking sleepy from her travels.

We cleared the table, and I waited for Siljan to say she was going upstairs to bed. I would follow her and tell her goodnight. Instead, she announced her desire to retire and Pahpee asked me to wash the dishes and prepare the kitchen for breakfast. The Swedish model bid us good night and went to her room. For an hour I washed pots, pans, plates, silver ware, glasses, thinking only of the latest guest, her attractive smile, and the wonderful meal we had all shared. My expectations of telling her goodnight fallen flat, the kitchen spotlessly cleaned, I climbed three flights of stairs to my bed, unable to see anything but her white hair against that black dress.

Once in bed, the room darkened, I glanced at the wall beside me. To my surprise, the moon was full and bright enough to reflect the image of the thick, round window pane on my wall. The moon was just coming up on the horizon, so the small, sharply focused patch of light was high on the wall. I watched the circular light pattern for some time, thinking of Siljan, below me, and wondered if the moon was casting the same design on her wall. I hoped it was. I fell asleep, hoping it was.

The next morning I awakened much too late to help with breakfast. I suppose as a good reward for my late night cleaning, Nanna or Pahpee had already washed the morning dishes and put things away. At least I didn't have to face the roasted tomatoes, yet again.

I had pulled on cotton shorts printed in a purple and green paisley pattern, a white tee shirt, and white canvass tennis shoes. Out to the barn to help feed the animals, I found

Siljan talking with Pahpee, looking at one of the horses. I remember that Pahpee suggested we could have gone for a ride, but that the other horse had had an infection in a hoof, leaving only one animal to ride. Siljan spoke right up.

"Mr. Briscoe, I don't mind sharing the horse. Can two people ride her?"

"I suppose, but you can't gallop her. You'll have to just walk her. Don't let her get hot and sweaty."

"Just who was my grandfather talking about?" I thought.

"Sure, I think Nathan and I can do that. We'll take real good care of her. We won't push her at all."

"You can ride down the path to the River Stour, Nathan knows the way. Right Nathan?" My grandfather looked at me with a smile, silently daring me not to return Siljan with any of her clothes missing.

"Yes sir, I know the way. And we'll go slow."

"That's right, real slow," the old man shot back, shaking a finger at me, out of Siljan's sight.

"I'm going to load up the other horse and take her into the vet. The sores on her leg are looking poorish. Back in a while."

I stuck my foot in the stirrup, and swung up behind the tall, erect posture of Christina Siljan. The curvature of the horses back forced us to sit very close, touching, in fact. Siljan, who had had some experience with horses through modeling, gave the reins a soft snap and the horse took us out through the gate which Pahpee had left open.

My hands felt awkward. Was I suppose to rest them on my legs? Put them behind me on the horse's rump? Or in front, around Siljans tight waist? Almost immediately, and honestly without any preconceived notion or planning of what was about to happen, I could tell my hands weren't going to be the only awkward part of this situation. The movement of the horse, my thin shorts, and the closeness of my body to Siljan's was not going to work, at least not without some embarrassment on my part. Even before we hit the end of the driveway, to cross the small road to the glen, I felt an incredible tingle in my groin. I began to shake, perhaps out of fear, maybe out of just being with this women who was probably twice my age and who I had already found to be extremely attractive.

"Nathan, are you all right back there?"

"Uh, yes, I think so. I'm just shaking for some reason."

"Are you cold? Sick?"

"No, don't think so, but I'm shaking very badly. I feel like I may fall. Any second, uh, I'm really think I should..."

With that, I quickly slipped off the right side of the horse, getting slightly ahead of Siljan, near the horse's head.

"Here, I'll help lead you!" I grabbed the reins and led the horse across the road, being sure I stayed well ahead of the Swedish model with long white hair, now gently wafting in the air.

Once crossing the road and heading down the trail things began to relax a bit.

"The purple flowers are phlox. The river is called the Stour. It connects with the Avon down the road toward Ilmington. The Avon flows through Stratford," I rattled off, starting a geography lesson to steer my thoughts away from the tension I felt.

"Yes, I know, I ate lunch yesterday on the banks of the River Avon. I shared my leftover bread with several swans. It is a beautiful place."

"Are you on vacation, or doing modeling work in England?"

"I wish I could say I was here to do work. I suppose you could say I am on holiday."

"When do you have to be back in Sweden?"

"Well, not too soon, at least for work. I plan to stay two more nights at Hope's Croft and then perhaps return home going through Denmark. Sometimes there is work in Copenhaven."

"*Sometimes* there's work there. I don't understand?"

"Nathan, let's not worry with work right now. It's too pretty today." It was obvious that Siljan did not want to talk about work. It didn't sound like she even had any work lined up at all. Soon, we were at the river and Siljan climbed down to let the horse have a drink. We tied the horse to a small willow tree and sat down near the same spot I had, just a day or two earlier, visited with the Venetti twins. The water looked cool, running lazily, the sky almost royal blue with a few puffy white clouds drifting and changing shape slowly; a bird somewhere singing a sweet summer tune.

What happened next, just, well, happened next. Siljan, sitting only a foot from me, placed her hand on my leg, just above my knee and below my shorts. She turned and looked at me. Her eyes reflected the blue sky, her hair the clouds, and her soft touch warmed my skin. Goose bumps raised in a random pattern up and down my legs. She saw the response, leaned over a bit further, and kissed me tenderly on the lips. We stopped, I kissed her back. I guess you could say the third time was an equal kiss. It was the first time in my life a girl, woman, had kissed me. I didn't shake at all from this point on.

She told me I was one of the most handsome young men she had ever met. It seemed odd to me that out of all the handsome young men in Sweden that she had ever met, that on this day, the "most handsome" was from Bethlehem, Pennsylvania. I couldn't think of anything grown-up to say, so I just said what I felt, "You are really beautiful, Siljan." That was all Christina Siljan needed. All she wanted was a handsome young man telling her how beautiful she was. It was apparent to me then, that what ever success Siljan had enjoyed in her younger days was now gone. She had been used up. Designers, promoters, agents had gotten what they wanted. They had moved on to other, younger models, and now Christina Siljan was alone. Worthless. Unneeded.

We held hands, kissed more, and laid back on the grass, enjoying the beautiful, late morning beside the River Stour. In a short while she got back on the horse, I climbed up behind her, and we silently guided the horse back through the phlox covered glen, across the road, up the driveway and into the barn, my hands gently wrapped around her waist the entire way. This time, I knew where to put them. Once there, I slid off the horse and helped Siljan down. We crawled up into a small loft above one end of the centuries old, long rock barn, taking the blanket with us, and lay in the hay. Soft rays of morning sunlight drifted through a small, open door in the gable, allowing us to see each other as we removed our clothes.

Soon, her dark Swedish body was tangled around mine and her long, white hair, hung over me, gently swaying. The air surrounding us both was filled with the sweet smell of early summer hay. As we moved together in the loft, the horse quietly shifting in her stall and eating wild oates below, I was christened into adulthood. No matter how long I live, I will never forget that single morning and Siljan's short stay at Hope's Croft. I will remember the smells, the feel, the love, everything. Everything so far removed from the everythings I had known before.

C H A P T E R   F I V E

Mr. Hope's Croft & Wife,

you have fun place. Real fun Place.

Mr. Sushimo & Friends.

幸福 を 祈ります。

The number of guests during my first week was small compared to the those we entertained the second week. A small group had made reservations to stay with us following several business days they had spent in London accompanied by sight-seeing in Stratford. In addition, Joe and Sandra Bledsoe, a retired couple from Alabama had planned a four night stay during the same period. Yes, it was indeed a strange mixture for the orange stone walls of Hope's Croft to cradle. But we survived, sort of, or at least most of the guests made it the duration of their planned stay.

Things got off to an interesting start when Joe and Sandra pulled up in the driveway, as I fed Larry and Lambkin just over the fence in the front yard. The couple was driving a rented Toyota, stuffed with suitcases, boxes of gifts, luggage, etc. Joe opened the back door of the dark gray Toyota and a number of bags and boxes fell out on the driveway.

"Dammit!" Joe spouted. "What the hell is all this junk, Sandra?"

"Joe, sweetheart, that brown box is loaded with Lladro's. They cost over twenty-five dollars a piece, please be more careful, sweetheart."

"What the...what is this?" Picking a strangely wrapped package up off the ground. Joe held up a free-formed shaped object about the size of several water melons and covered numerous times in plastic shopping bags, securely bound with gray duct tape. The large object rattled loudly as Joe shook it, as if it might contain some kind of glass, glass no longer in its original state.

"Joseph, you remember what that is? We bought it last week in Rome. My gosh, Joseph Bledsoe, it's the tabletop marble replica of the last supper. Miniature salt shaker included, mind you. Are you just too forgetful?"

"This is ridiculous. Two weeks of buyin' junk. Plain junk. The airline is gonna add a surcharge jest to get all this stuff back to 'Bama. I'm gonna loose about ha'f it before Friday."

"What's that sweetheart?"

"Nuthin'."

I finished putting several scoops of feed in the wood

trough just beyond the fence. Larry and Lambkin responded and were nibbling away, unconcerned about the tense conversation on the driveway.

"May I help you? I'm Nathan, the Briscoe's grandson?"

"Why sure 'nuff. We're the Bledsoe's. From Aler-bama, over in the US. Jest take these here two bags inside fer us and we'll be right behind ya."

Mr. Bledsoe was bald, dumpy, and wearing dark trousers with a "dip ring" on a back pocket made visible by countless boxes of round tobacco dip cans carried there for years. By his language alone it seemed obvious that he was from rural Alabama. And from the giant horseshoe-shaped diamond ring on his pinky finger he was rich as well. He wore a white dress shirt, long sleeved, but with the sleeves rolled up to his elbows. An old fashioned under shirt was clearly visible underneath, made so by a lot of sweat, causing its outline to show through the dress shirt. Mr. Bledsoe seemed to be one of those men who would sweat a lot, his cowboy boots probably always damp, maybe even in winter.

Mrs. Bledsoe wore a bright pink dress that came below her knees. On her feet were dark, flat shoes. She carried an oversized bag and often dug in it, for some time, looking for this or that.

From the first few moments in the driveway I could tell the Bledsoe's were one of those couples; the husband never happy with anything and the wife correcting absolutely everything her husband said or did, publicly, but in a semi-sweet way. Boy, was I looking forward to these guests.

"Where's do we sign in, young feller?"

"Right here, Mr. Bledsoe. Right here in the guest book. Just sign your name with today's date to the left. Feel free to add comments when you leave, also. I'll get my grand parents and let them know your here," I instructed, overhearing Mr. Bledsoe's next comment which he whispered too loudly as I went down the hall toward the kitchen.

"Nice kid, but he don't sound very British at all. Not at all!"

"Mr. and Mrs. Bledsoe, glad you have arrived. We received your recipes last month and I have been looking over them. We plan to fix you a homey southern American meal this evening. I think we have all the ingredients, accept perhaps, the mustard greens. I don't believe we have those available here, but we'll make a substitution. I hope you don't mind?" Nanna said, entering the hallway.

"No, not at all. But not just too way out, of a substitution, ya know. I have a very sensitive stomach. Just stick to sumpin' fried, and vegetables, if you don't mind," Joe responded.

"Yes, as I said, I did get the list. Oh, I have most unfortunate news for you. We have a group coming in a little later this afternoon and they will need the entire second floor, so I'll have to put you up on the third floor. Nathan sleeps up there, too. We hope you don't mind the stairs, if they are too burdensome for you to climb, there is a single person dumbwaiter back near the kitchen. Just let Mr. Briscoe know if you want to use it, instead. It's slow, but operable. You'll have to use it one at a time. It's a small lift."

I carried the Bledsoe's luggage upstairs and they followed

me to their room. Even though both appeared to be in their late sixties they maneuvered the stairs just fine. They took the room just down the hall from me, on the opposite side of the house. The room was called *Yarrow Flower*.

"Dinner will be at seven tonight. We will have quite a crowd, so seven sharp," I instructed the duo.

"Sure, 'nuff," Bledsoe replied.

Nanna had only told me a group would be coming around five in the afternoon and for me to stick close to the front yard to help with bags and room assignments. While cutting some daisies for the dinner table, a medium sized tour bus pulled into the driveway. From the door emerged half a dozen Japanese businessmen, all short, all black hair, all in white dress shirts, and maroon silk ties. The second their feet hit the driveway at Hope's Croft they chattered away. The six spoke Japanese at the same time, all six of them, and with the speed of light.

I greeted the men, they bowed ceremoniously to me, one at a time, to which I gave each a quick nod of my head, a sort of half-bow. They seemed friendly, but didn't want me to carry their things. They did that themselves. The bus left and I led them to the front door, Pahpee and Nanna were already there to greet them. One of the gentlemen was the leader and spoke a little English. The rest apparently could not speak English.

"Ahh, Meester Breescoe," the man said with a snap, "We are from Japanese stock market. We have reservation. You know?"

"Why, yes. You must be Mr. Sushimo. Happy to have you

here at Hope's Croft. Sign in, please. Nathan will take you to your rooms," Pahpee instructed.

I took the group to the second floor and simply gave them the four sets of keys and left the room assignments for them to make. I reminded,

"Dinner is at seven PM, in the dining room, down the stairs and to the left," I said showing him the number "seven" on my watch.

"Dinner, seven?" Sushimo repeated, I nodded agreement.

"See you," I added.

Mr. Sushimo folded his hands in front of his chest and bowed once again to me. This time, however, I bowed back, more fully, and he seemed to like that. Several of his companions saw my effort and they, too, came to me and bowed, all followed by my bow in return to each of them. We bowed a lot.

Nanna had prepared southern food for the group the first night in honor of the Alabama guests. They had requested large fried chicken pieces, dipped twice in a batter recipe they had sent Nanna. The double dipping gave the chicken an extra crispy crust. Along with the chicken were mashed potatoes, creamy gravy, and sweet country-style creamed corn and steamed white rice. Lots of rice. They had requested greens but Nanna could not locate those, so spinach was substituted. Promptly at seven all eleven of us converged on the dinning room. The table had been expanded by Pahpee to accommodate the group.

"Please have a seat," Pahpee instructed to the Bledsoe's.

"Are we suppose to eat with *all these folks*?" Mr. Bledsoe

quizzed Pahpee semi-softly.

"Of course, there's room for all of us."

Bledsoe looked around suspiciously as if eating with the Japanese businessmen might some how contaminate him and his wife. They sat down on one end, reluctantly. Quickly, the Asian men followed right behind, sitting closely to the Bledsoe's. Nanna brought out the chicken.

"Ahhh, chicken, sweet and sour?"

"No, Mr. Sushimo. Just chicken. Fried chicken. Fried like they do in southern America. No sweet and sour sauce."

Out came the potatoes.

"Ahh, whaaaat?" Sushimo's' voice curiously slowing down.

"These are mashed potatoes, Mr. Sushimo. Try them. Ask your friends to try them," Pahpee encouraged.

Then came gravy, creamed corn, and corn bread.

"Now this is a meal," Mr. Bledsoe commanded, patting his impressive belly.

"What, gravy?" Sushimo asked, and Mr. Bledsoe jumping in for the explanation.

"Ya see, little guy, ya take some of the left over fat, lard, from fryin' the chicken and then ya mix sum flour with it. You get it nice and hot, pour in a few cups of milk, salt and pepper, boil the hell out of it, and pour it right thar on your mashed 'taters and rice. Lordy, me, it's sum kinda eatin!"

Mr. Sushimo just stared at Bledsoe. Not a blink of his two coal black eyes.

"Well, GO...ON, EAT... IT!" Bledsoe repeated extra slow and extra loud as if that might some how complete the intercultural exchange that was taking place at the dinning table.

None of the six, trim looking Japanese men touched the gravy. However, Nanna brought out a big bowl of spinach and set it in the middle of the table. Steam rose off the hot greens.

"Ahhh, sea weed!" Sushimo observed.

"Well, no..." Pahpee started to correct, but since the only part of the meal that was sitting on the plates of the six Japanese men was chicken and plain rice, he left the confusion alone.

"Sea weed!" the Japanese men acknowledged as the bowl came around.

"Damn, Sandra, they think these here greens is sea weed. Ain't that a kick in the ol' britches?"

After everyone completed dinner Nanna beckoned the group to the patio for tea and dessert. Tea was served hot which delighted the Japanese, but irritated Mr. Bledsoe who complained that no one in Europe understood American iced tea habits. I had to agree with him. After dessert, the group retired and readied for bed.

A knock on my door came while I was lying on the bed writing my mother a post card.

"Ahhh, sir..." One of the Japanese men said, wrapped only in a white towel and rubbing his underarm as if to be taking a shower.

"Do you need a bathroom?" I asked rubbing my underarm, as well.

I got off the bed and showed the guy where the overflow bathroom was down the hall. I shut the door behind him, but never heard the knob lock. "Oh, well," I thought.

The note to my mother was short. I told her I was having a lot of fun and mentioned the Venetti sisters. I did not say anything about Siljan. Pahpee had given me some stamps and I placed one on the card and set it on my dresser to be mailed the next day. I slipped on shorts and a tee-shirt for bed and waited for the second floor guest to leave the third floor bathroom. After the water went off I stood in my doorway, tooth paste and tooth brush in hand, waiting, but then was surprised as Mrs. Bledsoe emerged from her room directly across from the bath. Talking nonstop, she said her husband had been in the ensuite bathroom for an hour and she could not wait any longer for her bath.

"Nathan, sweetheart, I really need to use the hall bath, can you please wait to brush your teeth? Thank you sweet heart," she said, without so much as looking up and opening the unlocked, but closed bathroom door.

I moved toward the bathroom door thinking maybe I should go ahead and quickly tell Mrs. Bledsoe that someone else might be in there. At the door, I paused and considered knocking. But, as my hand raised to the door I could hear the loud swoosh of the shower curtain being slid back with gusto. Instantly, I heard two loud screams.

"Yee-Auh-Yoo-Noooo!"

"My Gawd! Oh, My Gawd!"

I stood back away from the door hoping not to be knocked down by whom ever dashed out of the overflow bath, first. I heard more screams.

"Yoooh, noooh!"

"Joe. Joe Bledsoe. Come here nowwww!" Joe Bledsoe did not respond. I thought to myself, why doesn't one of them come out. Then it occurred to me that they were both likely stark naked. The Japanese man behind the shower curtain with no clothes or towel and Mrs. Bledsoe franticly trying to put something, anything on so she could get out of the bathroom. Finally, the door opened.

"Mrs. Bledsoe!" I said not knowing what else to say.

"There is a man in that shower. Stark necked. He was just standing there looking at me, while I was stark..."

The old lady looked at my puzzled face and stopped short of revealing that she, too, was "stark naked." She stomped across the hall to her door and turned the knob with stifled enthusiasm. Nothing happened. Absolutely nothing. She stood there, frozen facing her own door, the knob in her hand, eyes fixed on the brass name plate, *Yarrow Flower*.

"Young man, Nathan I believe, it appears that my door locked automatically when I left a moment ago. Could you PLEASE get me a key, NOW!" She ordered.

"Yes ma'am!" I flew downstairs to the key box to get another key to *Yarrow Flower*. Finding it quickly, I dashed back upstairs just in time to see her door close. Joe must have heard the commotion. As I stood there, brass skeleton key in hand, the bathroom door opened.

"Ahhh...Ohhh..." And a bow came from the nervous, wide-eyed Japanese businessman grasping the white towel tightly around his firm, little body. He bowed at me, held his towel even tighter, looked quickly left and right to make sure "she" was gone from the hallway and flew down the stairs to his own territory, bowing at me several more times as he descended, as if the ritual might make everything OK. I took a few steps back and could hear Mrs. Bledsoe giving Mr. Bledsoe the riot act. Poor guy.

The next morning I came to the traditional English breakfast table and counted the Japanese men. One, two, three,...six! They were all here and I could not tell which one it was. All smiled and bid me "good mornings" in Japanese sounding English, bowing slightly from their seats.

"Good morning," I answered back, smiling, wondering which one it was. Mr. Bledsoe, too, was already seated at one end of the table complaining that his false teeth were missing from the hall bath room were he had accidentally left them the previous evening. The sight of Mr. Bledsoe's puckered lips was too much.

Pahpee brought in portions of the English breakfast. Nanna followed him and everything was on the table ready for us to eat. Oh yes, one empty seat was located next to Mr. Bledsoe.

"Good morning to all, hope you found your sleep satisfactory," Nanna announced looking at the empty tall-back chair. "Where's Mrs. Bledsoe?"

"She's still 'ixin' hersel' a bit. I'm sure she'll join us, *all* of us real soon," Bledsoe said, mumbling, not able to say "f's" without his false teet.

"He knew," I thought. That meant at least four people were aware of the bathroom adventure from the night before. The Bledsoes, me, and him. Which one was him?

As the toast came around in the handy wire toast carrier,

she strolled into the room and took her seat. Several good mornings were directed toward Mrs. Bledsoe, who just sat quietly. You might think at first that she would avoid all eye contact with the six Asian guests. But she didn't. She picked up her coffee and, with each sip, stared at each Asian, one at a time. She stared at them long and hard watching their reactions. She had begun her search with Mr. Sushimo, sitting directly across from her. No reaction, just a smile. It was impossible to tell which man it was from just looking at them, they were all so identical. But she kept looking nevertheless. Looking deeply into the eyes of the man who must have seen her wrinkled old nude body as that shower curtain flew open. Each of them startled at what both cultures, American and Asian alike, find so secretive and personal: nudity.

Strange, however, because neither was on their own turf. They were in a third party culture, and in a shared community bath at that. She continued, one-at-a-time, looking into their dark eyes, waiting for a clue, watching for a hint of guilt; instead each face smiled and nodded to her attentiveness. At last, she came around the end of the table, past Pahpee, past me, to the man seated just to my left and right beside her. She turned her head and looked straight at the little man with black hair. He never looked up. He just kept on eating.

She moved her gray head down toward the table to look back up at the man who was chewing nervously on a greasy English sausage. The closer her face got to his, the faster he chewed. Her head now only inches from the side of his face, the Asian man looked obediently down at his own plate. Without blinking or moving her gaze from the man's face,

Mrs. Bledsoe picked up a tray of roasted tomatoes sitting in front of her, eased back slightly, and moved the tray to her lap. Like one cat staring down another, the old lady from Alabama repositioned the tray over her intercultural neighbor's lap, under the table, and titled the tray of warm mushy fruit toward him, spilling the entire platter of red yuck onto his lap. The man never moved. Not an inch. He just kept on eating breakfast. In disgust, Mrs. Bledsoe slid her chair back, stood, and marched out of the dining room.

Mr. Bledsoe jumped up and followed her out with his normal, "Mhat the hell?" unable to say an "w" without teeth.

Nanna and Pahpee watched the entire affair in disbelief. Five, of the six, Japanese men stared at the sixth who just sat quietly crunching on a piece of toast, not complaining or interrupted in the least by the whole event. The sound of a tomato plopping on the hard wood floor beneath him could occasionally be heard. But no one moved to do anything. In fact, everyone finished eating breakfast as if nothing had happened. It wasn't until the meal was over that Nanna and I cleaned up the mess, and observed that this was the second time that tomatoes had ended up inappropriately on the floor at Hope's Croft since my stay had begun, and a situation that had begun to cause her some concern.

In a short while, Mr. and Mrs. Bledsoe came down stairs, went out the front door and climbed into their rented Toyota. Not gone for good, as their belongings were still in *Yarrow Flower*, but apparently gone into Stratford to sight-see, perhaps to find a new B&B? New false teeth?

It was not surprising all this happened to the guests from

Alabama, as the name of their room, *Yarrow Flower* had quiet a legend. Early English botanists called the Yarrow plant "nosebleed" because when its leaves are put into one's nose, it causes bleeding. Of course, the Scottish still use an extract of the plant as an ointment to heal wounds. It appeared that this "Yarrow" wasn't healing anything at Hope's Croft.

Actually, the Japanese guest was in the bathroom *first*, and Mrs. Bledsoe simply walked in unannounced. Perhaps she should have knocked first. After all, the door was shut, the room steamy. In the end, this was the way of life not only at Hope's Croft but many B&B's in general. Isn't that why people enjoy staying in them? The desire for a sense of homi-ness, a personal touch, an appreciation for being a guest, almost like family is what attracts people to a B&B. Did then, still does.

Soon, the businessmen boarded their bus which had been sent to take them into Stratford. I hung around the front porch waiting on the mail carrier who usually came shortly before lunch. I was feeding Larry and Lambkin when the small mail truck pulled up at the road. I waved my arms to get his attention, so I could mail the post card to my mother. We exchanged mail, I waved good-bye and headed back up the driveway. In the stack of letters was one addressed to me. The return address was noted, "Christina Siljan, Stockholm, Sweden."

I rushed up the drive, excited. Excited that she had kept her word about writing me, and exuberant over what words the letter would contain. I went inside, left the rest of the mail on the guest table, took my letter upstairs to *Foxglove* and closed the door tightly behind me. I sat on my bed.

I opened the letter carefully not to hurt the return address. I pulled out the letter and began to read:

My Dearest Nathan,

And how does this fine English day find my good friend Nathan? Wonderful, I hope.

The week which has passed since I left Hope's Croft seems endless. Each day is a painful reminder that I can no longer see you. How wonderful it would be if if you could come to Sweden and see where I live.

When I returned to Sweden, I had hoped there would be work for me, but days have passed with no calls. Thoughts of you, dear Nathan, keep me positive. You gave me hope that someone still needs me. Maybe a call will come today. I shall wait.

I do hope when you receive this letter, Nathan, you too will fondly remember our time together. Please write to me and tell me what you are doing and about the new guests at the Croft. Write and tell me that you have thought of me.

Love, Christina Siljan

I moved over to the window and reread the letter from Siljan again. I read about how she missed me. About how I made her days exciting. About her lack of work and her constant thoughts of me. An invitation to see her. How could I go? How could I explain to Pahpee and Nanna that I needed to go to Stockholm, Sweden. That would never work, I knew it, but I reread about her desire for me to come anyway. Each word, each sentence, each thought made my heart race, my stomach bubble up in joy. I tingled.

I rushed to the bath room and sat on the floor. Sitting there, against the door, I reread the letter again. Hearing someone outside in the hall, I folded the letter back into the envelope. Looking up, I could see a hole under the sink. The hole was in the wall under the sink behind the bowl where the water pipes went into the wall. I stuck the letter into the hole on top of a wood stud, just below the pipes. My letter would be safe in its secret spot. I flushed the toilet so that it would appear I had been in the bathroom for a reason and then left, bumping into Mrs. Neeps on the way out.

Mrs. Neeps was about twenty-five years old and worked for Nanna and Pahpee. She lived just down the road and walked to work. A friendly woman, she would help clean the rooms when the B&B had a lot of guests. It was too much work for my grandparents alone. Mrs. Neeps would pull off the sheets, collect the towels and lower them down to the first floor on the single-person dumb waiter. On this day, Mrs. Neeps collected all the linens from the third floor and I helped her load them on the lift. I asked her if I could ride the lift down to the first floor with the linens and she agreed. I climbed in, she shut the door and flipped a switch in a box near the opening. The lift began to move slowly and down the shaft I went. There was not a light in the lift so I could see only by a small amount of light coming in through narrow openings as I passed each floor. It was neat.

The lift stopped automatically on the first floor and I waited for Mrs. Neeps to join me and let me out, which was necessary as there was no way to open the doors from the inside. Soon, I could hear her yelling, "Oh Nathan, Neeps is coming to save you. Hold on for a moment!"

She arrived, a little breathless, and the doors opened. I fell out, clowning as usual and helped her unload all the towels and things. I helped her carry them to a large cart she used to take the linens back to her house which was just down the road. She didn't have a car and the cart worked well, on non-rainy days. If it rained Pahpee would pick up the towels and sheets in his car. I followed her outside and she asked if I was busy. I wasn't and so she asked me to follow her home to get the shortbread.

"Shortbread?" I asked.

"Yes, of course! I forgot the bloomin' things back at me kitchen."

"Sure, I'll come with you."

I walked beside Mrs. Neeps who lived in a small cottage only a few houses down the road. Once at her small, rock-faced house she asked me to help carry in the towels. The woman thanked me and gave me two giant tins that contained her own homemade shortbread.

"It's me special recipe. Hope has her own, too. But when

she has a house full, she likes for me to make some extra. So if you will kindly take these back, don't eat them all up on your way, mind ya, and give them to Hope. You'll save Neeps another trip," Mrs. Neeps said, staring deeply into my eyes.

"Of course. Thanks," I said wondering about her look.

I stepped out the door of the tiny rock home and bid Mrs. Neeps good-bye again, but feeling as if she wanted me to stay. Once out on the road and out of sight, I pried open the lid of one for the tins and snuck out a shortbread cookie. I had never tasted anything like it back home. Later, Mrs. Neeps shared her short but sweet recipe with me to take back to Pennsylvania, though I must admit at some point both the recipe and desire to make the cookies disappeared with age. Best I remember the recipe went something like this:

Take slightly more than two sticks of real unsalted butter, to which you add two and one-half cups of sifted flour, and a half-a-cup of extra-fine sugar. Add flavoring, if desired. Mix together with a pastry blender until blended evenly into little pieces. Form a dough ball, cover with wax paper, and roll out into a flat circle with rolling pin, like a pizza crust, about one-half inch thick. Remove wax paper, use a pastry wheel or knife to lightly score into wedges, then prick the surface with a fork using your own pattern. Bake at 300 degrees on a lightly greased cookie sheet for 30 to 45 minutes, or lightly brown. Once cooled, the shortbread can be broken into separate wedges. Nanna was a great cook, but even she observed that Mrs. Neeps's recipe was the best shortbread to be found in all of England or Scotland.

Before I reached the front door of Hope's Croft with Mrs.

Neeps's full tins, I had eaten about half the shortbread from one of the containers. I placed the remainder on the island and hoped Nanna wouldn't be suspicious. She wasn't.

Later in the afternoon, the Bledsoe's returned from their outing. I wished the second they came in the front door they would announce an early departure. Instead, Mrs. Bledsoe entered the front door and asked me to "fetch" Pahpee, which I did. Pahpee had been working on a tractor and was trying to get grease off his hands when he came in and found Mrs. Bledsoe on the bottom of the stairs exhausted. Mr. Bledsoe had already gone upstairs.

"Yes ma'am, how may I assist you?"

"Mr. Briscoe, I am tired from walking all over Stratford, would you mind sending me up to the third floor on the elevator?"

"Of course. Follow me, the lift is back by the kitchen."

Mrs. Bledsoe followed my grandfather back to the kitchen with me right behind her. He opened the doors and she peered in. The tiny space was only about a foot-and-a-half square. The woman from Alabama wasn't way over weight, but she had no doubt enjoyed her daily portions of southern cooking over the years. She stepped inside the cubicle, her body touching all three sides.

Pahpee closed the doors securely and told me to go up to the top floor and open the doors once the lift had stopped. Off I ran up the stairs, the hum of a straining electric motor vibrating in the walls of Hope's Croft. I made it to the top in no time and waited for Mrs. Bledsoe. Somewhere, while passing through the second floor, a piece of the lift hung inside of the shaft. Apparently one of the top corners was off balance, perhaps by the cargo, and hung on a support board inside the wood shaft. The tension caused the motor to work even harder and finally, unexpectedly, it over heated and shut off. The hum through out the house turned to silence except for the sound of Mrs. Bledsoe's inquisitiveness.

"Hell-o. Mr. Briscoe, are we there yet? Hell-o!"

I could hear Pahpee down below.

"Mrs. Briscoe are you on the third floor? Nathan, do you see her?"

"Uh, no sir, she's not up here. I think I can hear her below me, Pahpee," I informed.

Pahpee rushed upstairs to me, and asked,

"Mrs. Bledsoe, can you hear me?"

"Why, yes, sweetheart, I can. Are we there? Would you open the door?"

"No, I don't think you are quite here, yet. Hold on."

My grandfather and I then went down to the second floor and discovered that she was stuck in between floors. Mrs. Bledsoe, queen of the bathroom stormers, depositor of slushy tomatoes on her enemy, was stuck somewhere between the second and third floors. About this time, the Japanese businessmen arrived back from their trip to Stratford. They came up the stairs to find Pahpee and I talking to the wall...and being answered. Five of the Asians stared at the wall as if it were haunted, the sixth, recognizing the stressed woman's voice inside dashed for his room. He did not wish to be any part of the current affair involving Mrs. Bledsoe.

"Mrs. Bledsoe, I think I can get you out, but I need you

to stay calm."

"Mr. Briscoe, I think you just need to concentrate on getting me out of this elevator thing, NOOOOW!"

Pahpee went back down stairs to get a screwdriver. The door would not open if the elevator was not at the correct position so he would have to force the second floor doors open. Quickly, he came back up and unscrewed the cover off the switch box, and disconnected some wires. He placed the screwdriver between the doors until a small crack appeared. He motioned for the five Japanese men to stick their fingers in the crack and help force the doors open. I helped, too.

With all seven of us pulling the doors apart, they finally released and there we could clearly see Mrs. Bledsoe, or more accurately, Mrs. Bledsoe's feet and lower legs. Her legs from the knees down were above our heads. All seven of us stood on the second floor looking up the shaft into, well, up into Mrs. Bledsoe's dress until we all realized where we were looking. She too, at this point, realized the same thing, her clue was several of the Asian's observations,

"Ahhh, yes, ahhh!"

You could tell from the nonverbal reaction of Mrs. Bledsoe's lower legs that she wanted to somehow pull her dress down around her calves, though that was impossible given the tight space in which she was confined. Pahpee quieted everyone.

"Mrs. Bledsoe, can you sit down on the floor of the lift?"

"I don't know, I'll try."

The old lady attempted to crouch in the elevator but was unable to go any lower when her posterior lodged up against the back wall of the lift. Now she was stuck.

"Mrs. Bledsoe, are you all right? Can you move?" Pahpee asked hoping for a positive answer.

"No sir, I can not move up or down now. Thank you, sweetheart."

"Well, let's see. Nathan, go get a ladder from the barn and hurry back."

I responded with great speed bringing the ladder to Pahpee's feet.

"Gentlemen," Pahpee said adjusting the ladder in front of the opening, "we are going to have to pull Mrs. Bledsoe out of the lift by her feet and legs.

"Aaah, oooh!" the five responded as Pahpee motioned how we were going to maneuver the lady out of the stuck lift.

"Mrs. Bledsoe, just stay still."

"Pardon me?"

"So sorry, just, just be calm, we are about to get you out."

With that, Pahpee lined all of us along each side of the ladder, himself on top and grabbed Mrs. Bledsoe's feet. She screamed. He pulled. She screamed again. He kept pulling until her legs were sticking out into the room. He passed off her feet to the first two of us while he stayed underneath supporting her body as it emerged. Now, her knees were visible as we inched her out of the shaft. More of her legs were exposed as we passed the lady along the line, Mrs. Bledsoe being delivered into the room much like a baby out of a birth canal. Would she be just as angry as she was this morning, once she was out?

Pahpee supported Mrs. Bledsoe's back end and then

finally her back. Three of us on one side supported her, three on the other. We held her much like you would a coffin, only she was very much alive. Pahpee held Mrs. Bledsoe's head as it came out of the shaft and supported it as he climbed down the ladder. All of us moving along her body, finally placing her feet on the floor and standing her up straight.

Once on her feet the woman didn't say a word. Not even "thank you". She took a step forward, then another, and disappeared up the stairs to her room. We wanted to cheer, but it didn't seem appropriate for the moment. The Japanese went to their rooms, and Pahpee and I carried the ladder back down stairs holding back giant guffaws.

I went out to the barn with Pahpee, embarrassed about the whole situation with Mrs. Bledsoe. Later a car drove off around the front and we could see the Toyota going down the road. I went inside and found this handwritten entry in the guest book:

Hope's Croft,

<u>Not</u> for us!

Joe and Sandra Bledsoe

Alabama

It is probably best that the Bledsoe's went ahead and departed early, as they would have certainly been distraught over the traditional Japanese meal planned by Nanna that evening.

She had worked most the afternoon on a forty-five pound Sea Bass, that was delivered on ice along with some other special items from a fresh food market in London. Nanna had stuffed the giant fish with mushrooms and walnuts. The bass, almost three feet long, barely fit in the large commercial oven.

Nanna had Pahpee and me prepare a long table made of stacked bales of hay, topped by a large antique wood door that had been stored in the barn. The door was cleaned, but left bare. No table cloth was used.

The table was positioned in the middle of the large bricked patio which had been strung with several small kerosene lamps by Pahpee. Oriental music of some kind played on the stereo that Nanna asked me to set up. Freshly sliced pineapples, kiwi, and oranges had been lined up on large banana leaves which had arrived along with the delivered fish. Giant bowls of rice, both steamed white rice and darker fried rice, were placed on either end of the table. Wood trays were filled with large purple grapes, plums, and small bunches of bananas. A variety of sushi...wrapped in true seaweed, not spinach, was set out.

Dinner was served at seven o'clock and the six Japanese guests enjoyed all the extra work we did to make the evening memorable. The giant bass, presented on the largest of all of Nanna's trays was bordered in fancy lettuce. The head of the fish was still intact, a custom Nanna said Japanese preferred. The evening was a real Asian festival, so peaceful and fun, compared to the previous night. Late in the evening the Japanese men retrieved a bottle of *sake* from upstairs. One of the them, I feel certain it was the one who endured Mrs. Bledsoe's hot tomato bashing, got most inebriated. He had earned the opportunity.

The event on the patio was my first real understanding of what purpose Hope really had for the Croft. After forty years *she* understood thoroughly. But this was my first glimpse. To me, she wanted it to be a gathering place were people of different cultures would stay, relax, and enjoy the unplanned chance of luck system of people sharing their food, experiences, and friendships. Each week, each stay, was a different experience for all, and the whole process was held together by my grandmother, Hope.

❊❊❊

Every day at Hope's Croft was like a new birthday celebration loaded with presents. And the events and experiences of the weekly celebrations were topped only by those of the following week. I turned several pages of the 1962 guest book to find the July entry of a beautiful young girl from Australia, traveling with her parents. An interesting couple from India also visited during the same period. These visitors, along with Mrs. Neeps, continued to stretch the boundaries of my self-awareness.

CHAPTER SIX

> Our Friends at Hope's Croft,
>   How relaxing these few
> days have been as your guests.
> the foods, the Purple Phlox
> hillsides, picnics by the
> River Stour, it's all
> wonderful! And, by the way,
> Dinny adores Nathan.
>   Thanks for a great time
> in the Cotswold Hills.
>   The Albrittons
>   Lance, Julia and Dinny

I remember Lance and Julia Allbritton as being the coolest adults I had ever met, not to mention their daughter,

Ginny, whom I still remember very fondly. The Albritton's lived on the coast of Australia, just north of Sydney. Their Aussie accent fit right in with Nanna's and Pahpee's. Lance was a tall man, several inches taller than me, and had longish blonde hair (long for an adult in the early sixties). He looked like he might have just stepped away from a massive sail boat, as its captain, though in reality he *was* connected to the seas. He owned a large sailing and ship accessory outfitting store in Gosford.

Ginny's mother Julia worked in a travel office, which is how she knew of Hope's Croft. She found the B&B listed as possible accommodations for tourists traveling in the Stratford, England area. As Mrs. Allbritton told us during our first breakfast together, she had made reservations for a customer to stay at the B&B, the summer before and the client came back raving about the place, the food, and Hope.

The Allbritton's were the only guests their first night and then were joined by a couple from India during the last part of their stay. They had arrived late in the evening on the first day, long after dinner, and so I only caught a glimpse of Ginny as they checked in. Her long blonde hair had obviously come from her father and she was tall and slender like him, too. Ginny's facial features were sharp and strong, but not in a manly way. Her features seem to say, "I've got character." Her eyes were brown. She was quite simply, beautiful.

The parents stayed in *Evening Primrose* and Ginny's room was, *Columbine*, both on the second floor. Ginny's room was almost entirely furnished in white country wicker. *Columbine* was perhaps the most innocent and sweet looking room at

Hope's Croft. The room fit Ginny Allbritton from Australia to a tee. Her bedspread was a multi-colored print of every wild-flower imaginable. Under each wildflower printed on the spread was its botanical name. To carry out the theme, Hope had hung framed dried wild flowers from her own flowerbeds on the walls. As the centerpiece, she had had a local photographer take extreme close-ups of one summer's crop of wild-flowers and had the photos framed and matted in a large collage. At the bottom, right corner of the mat the words, "Hope's Flowers, Summer 1958" had been penciled.

To me, *Columbine* had just been another room on the second floor, a space for one of the six Japanese men to call home for a few days. But after the Allbrittons arrived, *Columbine* became sacred ground. My curiosity of what went on in the room, how she looked sleeping in the bed, where she sat consumed my thoughts daily. Not in the way my interests were excited by Siljan, but in a more innocent manner. I would never have thought to "explore" Ginny" the way Siljan had allowed. Fact is, Siljan did most of the exploring for both of us. Ginny was different. Innocent.

Following breakfast after their first morning, I was asked by Nanna to help prepare a picnic basket for the Allbrittons. She said they had requested to have a picnic lunch out under the giant oak by the Stour. About ten AM I met Nanna in the kitchen and got out all the items she said we needed. A loaf of Oatmeal bread, mayonnaise, tomatoes, pickles, lettuce, and smoked turkey.

I sliced the bread into half-inch slices and coated each one with a thin spread of mayonnaise. On each went garnishments. Thin waxed brown paper was folded gently around each sandwich and secured with a red rubber band.

I was then asked to slice unpeeled oranges which were placed in a long, shallow pottery tray. This tray, and all the hand-thrown pottery at Hope's Croft, was marked on the bottom with either the name "Brown," or "Bucek." The items marked "Bucek," also contained two oriental symbols. The symbols, as Nanna informed me, were for prosperity and freedom. In preparing the oranges, the long tray I used was marked with the oriental characters.

While I was preparing the sandwiches, Nanna was putting together vegetable sticks, as she called them. She made stick people out of celery, small round tomatoes and sliced cucumbers. She held the stick people together with colored toothpicks. The clever vegetables were placed in a small wicker basket that had been lined with a navy blue batik cloth napkin. All of these items were placed in a large picnic basket made of grape vine. On one end of the big basket we placed a bottle of French white wine, three wine glasses made of pottery, and a small bottle of fruit juice. Cloth napkins slid through wood napkin rings and a large Scottish plaid tablecloth were also added to the basket. Three plates were added. Every time "three" of something was added to the basket I had wished Nanna was saying, "Four..." But she didn't. I even suggested they might need an extra cup or fork, but Nanna never responded.

Once the basket was properly packed Nanna asked me to go up to *Evening Primrose* and inform the Allbrittons that there basket was ready anytime they wished to pick it up. I went to my room and flopped on the bed wishing that there was a "forth" person on the picnic. Me.

I wished that somehow, I would be invited. Invited to be a friend of Ginnys. To help conversation along. To share about my life in the United States, my adventures at Hope's Croft. But no, I just laid on the bed. In a while I went back downstairs hoping that maybe the Allbrittons would need directions to the Stour. Sure, it was just a few minutes across the Phlox covered glen, but one would want the *right* tree. The one with the swing, of course.

I waited and waited. Finally, the family came down and Nanna tasked me to get the basket out of the cooler where it had been stored. I brought it to the dining room and waited in the study. The family retrieved the basket off the dining room table and headed out the front door of Hope's Croft. I raced to the door to see if they needed directions. No, they had picnicked on the river last summer.

Taking my seat by the chess board in the study, I looked out the window and could see the family passing by the wood fence. The three figures appeared distorted as I looked at them through the thick, round pane of glass in the study window. It was all over. I just sat.

I went out back to help Pahpee with the animals and to get feed for Larry and Lambkin. In a while I came around front and fed the waiting sheep. I kept saying in my mind over and over, "Ginny, come back and ask me to join you." Finally, I whispered it aloud several times. The truth is I wanted to shout it. Shout it so loud that she could hear me from the front yard of Hope's Croft, across the glen, and all the way down to the big oak tree by the Stour. No shout. No Ginny.

I took the empty bucket around to the barn, and thought about Siljan, about how she liked me. I thought about the loft just above me in the barn. I went back inside and sat on the island while Nanna worked on dinner. She took one look at me, slumping with my head in my hands, and asked,

"You must not have been invited to the party by the Stour?"

"How did you know?"

"While we prepared the basket you were insistent that they might need extra-this, extra-that. I've lived long enough to know, and entertained more than my share of love struck couples. I can tell when a gentlemen has an eye on his fancy. It wasn't easy putting the picnic lunch together knowing you weren't included, even though you dearly wanted to be. Nathan, I appreciate your willingness to help. You are a kind young man."

This was the first time in almost two weeks that my grandmother spoke to me in any way other than instructing me about my responsibilities. She was empathizing. How unique? Maybe now was the time to ask. Maybe she would be willing to discuss the events of my mother leaving twenty years earlier. It seemed so much so the correct moment, I phrased the question in my mind and started.

"Nanna,..." But before I got any further a voice behind interrupted,

"Excuse me, but my parents sent me back to see if Nathan would like to join us for lunch by the river?"

I practically fell off the island. A smile lit across my face and

I completely forgot my discussion with my grandmother.

"Of course. Sure, of course. Is it all right, Nanna?"

"But, of course," and she smiled. Both shes.

"Nanna, should I take an extra cup and plate?"

"Right there in the pantry, on the second shelf. And Nathan, there's a sandwich in the cooler. I just made them for you and Pahpee. Go ahead and wrap it up. You might need an extra apple or two."

I collected the items, put them in a large brown paper bag, and Ginny and I headed down the hall and out the front door. Along the way we talked bout our homes; back in Australia and in Pennsylvania. We talked about her "holiday" and the fact that I called it "vacation."

We strolled through the glen and the day was perfect. I was nervous and very anxious when I came down the same path just a few days earlier with Siljan. But not now. It was OK this time. I knew that we would never end up in the loft of the barn, either. But that was all right, too. With Ginny, I felt different, like I was the one in control.

Under the tree we were greeted by her parents.

"Nathan, glad you could join us," Mr. Allbritton said, standing and shaking hands with me, our heads almost banging into the lower tree limbs. "Have a seat."

"Thanks. I brought along some extra food so I don't eat up all the stuff in the basket," I awkwardly contributed.

"Just add it in, we'll all share and enjoy the wonderful food of Hope's Croft," Mrs. Allbritton directed, sipping wine from one of the pottery glasses.

"Have you enjoyed your holiday?" I asked, to appear

interested in the family as a whole and not just Ginny.

"Oh yes. My goodness we have spent three weeks on the Eurail. We've visited six countries," Mrs. Allbritton revealed.

"My favorite was Brugge," Ginny stated.

"Where's Brugge?" I asked

"Brugge is a small town not too far from Brussels. Brussels, Belgium," Mr. Allbritton explained.

"I'm not really sure where Belgium is..." I quizzed.

"Belgium is just across the Channel. France is to the south, Holland to the north. Germany borders the western portion of the country."

"Nathan, the town we visited, Brugge, has old cobble stone streets and canals, like Venice," Ginny added.

"Wow. It must be neat to visit all those places. Coming here is the first time I've been out of the United States. I've only been out of Pennsylvania, one other time."

"You've picked a pretty nice place to visit, Nathan," Mr. Allbritton reassuring me.

"I have great grandparents, but this is the first time I've ever met them face-to-face."

"This is the *first* time you've seen them?" Mrs. Allbritton asked, wanting a greater explanation from me.

"Yes, well you know, it's a long way from here to Pennsylvania and really expensive. Nanna and Pahpee are busy every day of the year. They almost never leave Hope's Croft. They have to be here for guests. If they left, who would prepare meals and entertain? Certainly not Larry and Lambkin. It would be a one-sided conversation." We all laughed as Pahpee pulls his "deaf" trick the moment guests step out of there cars.

"Julia, why don't we take a walk?" Mr. Allbritton suggested followed by a nod from Julia. They refilled their wine glasses, pulled themselves up off the red, green, and gold plaid Scottish ground cloth and began following the bank of the River Stour. I looked over at Ginny, she looked back.

"You have great parents. It's cool that they let you see all these different countries. You're lucky."

"Just wait until I do something wrong, they're not so 'cool' then," Jenny admitted, pulling a grape off a cluster and popping it in her mouth.

"I would like to see more places in the world. Just the past two weeks have opened my eyes. All I ever thought about before was about ten square blocks in Bethlehem, Pennsylvania. Even at first, I didn't want to come over here. I knew I would be away from my friends. But now. I am lucky, just like you."

"Nathan, you are so sweet. Tell me about your parents."

I choked here. Was I to lie? Should I just make up something? Did I want to get into why my mother had arranged for me to even be sitting here on the banks of the River Stour?

"My mother works for a steel factory, in an office, of course. My father...well Ginny...my father...he..."

"It's OK, Nathan. You don't have to tell me," she said.

I knew she thought I was probably going to say, "divorced," but I skirted the topic and simply said, "He's not living." The beautiful blonde girl from Australia reached over and took my hand and told me how sorry she was.

"Thanks, but it was a long time ago," I said and changing

the subject. "You know just a couple days ago I was jumping off the rope, there," pointing to the rope gently swaying in the light breeze. Maybe we should jump?"

"Oh Nathan, that would be so fab," Jenny said enthusiastically. When?"

"Let's ask your parents when they come back. Last week I jumped with these two...uh...really nice ladies from Italy. It was incredible," I said while Ginny grabbed my arm, shaking it, becoming more and more excited about the possibility.

I leaned back on the giant plaid cloth and looked up through the tree leaves at the sparkling sun rays thinking about all that had happened in my life the few, short days at Hope's Croft. How my mind had been exposed to so much newness. And now, laying back on this colorful spread with the most beautiful girl I had ever met in my life, it was almost too much. Who cared why my mother and Nanna were so crosswise with each other? My life, at the moment here in England, was terrific.

After a while, her parents rejoined us and we began packing everything back in the basket. Ginny asked her parents if we could jump off the rope and they agreed, but later, as they had planned a night at the theatre, and unfortunately for me, dinner in Stratford. It would be a long, long evening.

As the four of us walked toward the Croft a car was in the driveway and a dark-skinned couple was getting out. I introduced myself, and the Allbrittons followed behind. I helped the couple in with their luggage. Nanna came to the door when she heard familiar voices and threw her arms around the woman.

"You have made it safely, all the way from Bangalore, I see! Namastay! Namastay!"

"Namastay!" The woman returned.

" How was your trip?"

"Long, but pleasant," the short, dark-haired woman answered, her colorful silk dress material shimmering in the light.

"Did you meet the Allbrittons?"

"No, I am sorry."

"Lance and Julia Allbritton, their daughter Ginny, this is Rajesh and Vijaya Srinivas. They have come all the way from Bangalore, India. They are dear friends of ours, and have been for many years."

Everyone shook hands and retired to the study. I carried the suit cases upstairs to *Coneflower* and came back down. The couple from India sat on the sofa and the Allbrittons in the two leather chairs. Ginny was seated on a foot stool, Pahpee and Nanna were off to the kitchen to ready hors d'oeuvres. The Allbrittons would not be here for dinner, so this was the opportunity for the couples to chit-chat. I sat on the floor, near Ginny.

"How is India?" Mr. Allbritton asked.

"As I am sure you have read in the Australian newspapers, we have had many conflicts recently along the China-India border," Mr. Srinivas explained.

I looked at Ginny ignoring the "men's discussion."

"Britain has sent us arms and supplies, as has the United States, and it looks like we may finally be driving the Chinese back across the border," Mr. Srinivas continued.

I looked up when I heard "the United States" mentioned but otherwise was playing with a chess piece on the floor, out of sight from everyone but Ginny. It was a white knight. I was galloping it across the rug and the adventure was causing Ginny to chuckle. Soon, I made it jump over some of the other pieces. A pawn. A castle. The rook. The silliness made Ginny hold her hand over her mouth to keep from laughing out loud and disrupting the adult conversation which continued.

"As you know, Mr. Allbritton, with Ghandi's death only fourteen or fifteen years ago, even the Hindu and Moslems are still clashing. Up at Kashmir..."

I placed one of the kings on the back of the knight and galloped it around on the floor, playing like I was piercing some enemies with a lance, a single straw pulled from the nearby fireplace broom. Ginny placed her hand on her forehead, threw back her head as if in distress...and held a queen in her other hand near the floor.

"I don't know if the Moslems and Hindu people will ever make peace. There always seems to be bloodshed," Srinivas concluded, stopping to ponder the lengthening discussion.

"Sounds like what India needs is another hero, like Ghandi, a knight in shinning armor," Mrs. Albritton suggested.

I caught the last part of the conversation and took Ginny's hand — queen between fingers — and placed the queen on the back of the knight, just behind the king. Her giggles ceased to be giggles, and turned instead to an affectionate smile. If the room had been empty, we would have kissed. I know we would have kissed. There was a lull in the conversation and Pahpee brought in snacks, followed by Nanna who carried a tray of drinks. First the ladies and then the gentlemen took a drink and a snack.

"Nathan...," Mr. Albritton said with a sharp, determined voice causing me to spill my fruit juice in fear.

"Yes, sir?" Had he seen me playing chess with his daughter?

"Why don't you find us a game to play?"

"Well there's chess, but that would only be for two people. There are some games in the closet. What would you like to play? Scrabble?" I suggested getting up and not noticing the wet juice spot on my pants near my zipper.

"Here is a deck of cards and Scrabble," I confirmed, taking both to the center of the room as everyone, but me, noticed my wet pants.

"Uh, Nathan, my grandson, you must have sloshed your juice. Perhaps you should go change?" Pahpee suggested.

I looked down and was horrified. Dropping the games, I ran out of the room and upstairs. I changed into other pants and returned for the game of international Scrabble, which was fun because we used words from our own cultures, and so it was difficult to know if a particular word was really a word or not.

After the game ended, with Mr. and Mrs. Srinivas winning, the Allbrittons went to their rooms to get ready for their night out. How I wished I would be invited along but as Ginny explained, their theatre tickets had been purchased well in advance and performances were almost always sold out in the summer in Stratford. I would eat dinner with the

Indian couple and later, lie in my bed waiting to hear the car doors slam from an evening in Shakespeare's country.

Nanna served dinner promptly at seven PM. The table was set with several stew looking dishes, lots of yellow rice, and some flat things that looked like Mexican tortillas. No silverware had been set on the table, only plates.

The five of us gathered around the table and had a seat, Pahpee and Nanna on the ends, Mr. Srinivas on one side and his wife and I on the other. It was a strange seating, but that was arrangement. I looked for silverware thinking that Nanna, over-worked from the last few days must have forgotten it. No.

The Srinivases simply placed a large spoonful from each of the bowls on their plates and then took the flat, flour tortilla looking thing and pinched up small amounts of food. Basically, they were using the tortillas as a spoon or fork. I watched in disbelief, until everyone realized I had *not* done this before. There was a laugh and then Nanna explained we were going to eat the Indian meal the way many Indians eat...using the *roti* as a scoop.

"Go ahead," she instructed, to which I did. The food was somewhat hot and spicy with a lot of curry, saffron, and peppers. It was an interesting meal, consumed in an interesting manner. Afterwards, we visited some more and I watched as Pahpee and Mr. Srinivas rose from the table and walked toward the patio. There was a little light left, the sky almost purple, and the evening was cool. I followed them. Outside, Mr. Srinivas took Pahpees hand as my grandfather showed him the various flowers in the beds. After each examination of a particular flower, they held hands again. I was shocked by what I was watching. I wondered if Nanna knew what was going on. Was she looking out the kitchen window? Was my grandfather...?" I stared at them. After a few moments my grandfather noticed my intense stare.

"Nathan, what's wrong with you, why are you looking at me like that?"

"Well, Pahpee, you, you two were, well, holding hands?" My voice went up so as to sound more humorous than unhappiness with what I saw. Both men laughed.

"In India, Nathan, most men who are good friends hold hands. It does not mean anything sexual. Not at all. Just friendship."

"Well, we don't do that in Bethlehem, Pennsylvania. If we did, you'd turn the whole state into one big San Francisco!" The men laughed at my ignorance and lack of sophistication.

"Nathan, I doubt that. Besides, Mr. Srinivas and I have been friends for many, many years...and we are both happily married."

"Happily married to beautiful women," Srinivas added.

"Relax, grandson! Much of the world marches to a song with which you may not be familiar. It's only friendship. That's all."

I said OK and went back into the kitchen hoping I didn't see my Nanna and Mrs. Shrinivas holding hands. They weren't. Only laughing and washing the dishes. I went to my room and waited to hear car doors opening and shutting. I drifted off to sleep.

The next morning I was awakened by the sound of a

chant. A kind of rhythmic singing, over and over. I got out of bed and went to the hall. The sound seemed to be coming from the second floor, so I traced it down the flight of stairs. As I got closer, the voice was more clear. It was coming from *Coneflower*, and the door was slightly open. I listened and watched through the crack.

Mr. Shrinivas was on his knees, his body wrapped in a white sheet looking outfit that surrounded his mid-section. He was facing a small table that a clock and lamp normally rested upon but which was covered with purple silky material. On the table was a wood carving about eight inches high. The carving was of an elephant looking figure, but was also human looking, with human arms. On either side of the wood carving was fruit, cut in half, and a coconut. Leaves were scattered around the table top and two candles were burning.

Mr. Srinivas continued his chanting, not knowing I was standing at the door. I could not see his wife in the room. He raised his head and placed a finger on his right hand into a small silver container which I had never seen before. The finger then went to his forehead and a red dot remained between his eyes, just at the top of his nose.

The phrase that Mr. Shrinivas chanted seemed to be the same words over and over. Incense was burning somewhere in the room and I finally left, bewildered at what I had seen. Later, during the traditional English breakfast with all eight of us present, I got up the nerve to ask what he was doing.

"I was worshiping, Nathan," Srinivas responded. "I worship three times a day for about fifteen minutes. Mostly I am in prayer, in a special area called the *puja*."

"You seemed to be saying the same thing over and over..."

"Nathan, maybe Mr. Srinivas would rather eat his breakfast without a discussion of his...," Nanna gently corrected.

"No, Hope, it is OK. What I was repeating was my Mantra. I learned it when I was a young boy. I have recited the same Mantra three times a day for all of my life. It brings me closer to God. The Mantra has special powers," Mr. Srinivas patiently, kindly, and proudly explained to us all.

"The Hindu people are very religious and disciplined, Nathan," Mr. Allbritton added, obviously educated in Indian culture.

"I have a Hindu friend at my school," Ginny added.

"I've never met someone from India, at least not until I met both of you. I think it's neat that you are so dedicated to your religion. I know many people who are not," I reflected.

After breakfast, I helped clean the dishes, pots, and pans and then went out to the porch hoping Ginny might come out. She did, and her parents allowed us to go swimming by ourselves, which was a surprise. After we jumped from the ropes a dozen times each, we sat down by the Stour. We talked for a while about Mr. Srinivas and about own religious beliefs. After we had just about worn that topic out, with our bodies still glistening from drops of water from the River Stour, I leaned over and kissed Ginny Allbritton from Gosford, Australia. I kissed her on the lips and she kissed me back. I knew we had to stop there, so after the last kiss, I stood and challenged her to a race back to the Croft. I had no idea Ginny was on a track team at school. She beat me.

That evening while all the adults were in the study playing bridge, Ginny and I went out and sat on the lawn furniture in the front yard. The stars seemed much brighter at Hope's Croft than they ever did in Bethlehem. The lack of street lights and lighting from industrial buildings flooded the English sky with darkness, allowing the truth of other worlds to shine through brilliantly. Other worlds far out in space, as well as those only continents away.

As we sat on the white love seat I put my arm behind Ginny's neck, she leaned her head back, and we gazed toward the heavens. Like opposing magnets, our hands met in front and we turned toward each other. Our lips kissed once and then again. And then again and again. Her gentle hands stroked my face, my hand her soft blonde hair. In all my years since, I have never felt the way I did when I sat on that bench with Ginny Allbritton.

A day later the Allbrittons packed up and left. Like most guests at Hope's Croft, they left quickly right after the traditional English breakfast. I watched as Ginny got into their rented car and headed out of the driveway. I was beginning to not like standing in the driveway when guests departed.

We had exchanged our American and Australian addresses. I had a lump in my throat as I watched Ginny's car make the last turn out-of-sight down the country road toward Stratford. For some strange reason I can't explain, I never wrote her after I returned to Pennsylvania in August. She never wrote me, either. However, I am certain we both had good intentions of doing so.

❖❖❖

The message written in the guest book by the Shrinivas again aroused my curiosity about, "Namastay." Their entry read:

Our Dear Friends,

Once again, you have brought magic to our lives! At home, we face over-population, hunger, and filth. The political and Social Struggles go on endlessly. Yet, somehow, at the same time India is perhaps the most inter-connected civilization on Earth, proudly humming along like a giant organism, dependent upon each other for survival. Keep her in your Christian prayers.

Affectionately,

Rajesh & Vijaya

"NAMASTAY!"

C H A P T E R   S E V E N

One weekend in early August, Pahpee and Nanna were gone to visit a friend in London who was quite ill. They suggested that I come along with them, but I really didn't want to. Spending two days with someone I didn't know who was deathly ill did not sound fun, even in London. Besides, I had been at Hope's Croft all summer and felt safe, secure, and at home. I insisted that they go on to London. There weren't any guests anyway and things would be OK.

When you own a bed and breakfast establishment you can't always plan on reserved guests. And on those occasions when you don't want anyone stopping, for whatever reason, you simply put out the "No Vacancy" sign. Because I was alone for the weekend, Pahpee had placed the sign out by the road. But the sign didn't stop a tour bus which came to a slow stop on the country lane just in front of Hope's Croft. The bus, not terribly large, pulled off the narrow road and stopped at the end of the driveway. I had been sitting out on the front lawn love seat drinking a cup of hot tea when the bus pulled in.

I saw the driver get out and open the hood and then look underneath at the engine. Slowly, young men began stepping out of the bus. Each wore jeans and a German National Football (soccer) jersey. After a few minutes one of the men walked down the long driveway to the wood gate in the front yard. In a very heavy German accent he asked if he might use the telephone. I could see they were having a problem so I told him to come inside. He made a phone call to a bus company in London. I could tell from his response that no one on the other end picked up the phone. He hung up.

The man asked if we had a London phone book, but I had no idea where one might be. I never used one and had never seen Nanna or Pahpee use one either. We looked. Nothing.

"This is not good. Nah. Not good," the man said, sounding really upset.

"Maybe we could call an operator?" I suggested.

"An operator can not wake up the owner of the bus company this late. We are stuck. Where are we?"

"This is Hope's Croft. It's a bed and breakfast. But we're not open right now. My grandparents own it and they are, well, they're in London. We're closed for the weekend."

"We just came from a pub in Stratford."

"Are you a group, from...," curiously I asked from hearing his accent.

"My name is Gunter Frommer. I am one of the managers of the German National Football Team. A few days ago we completed competition in the Europe soccer finals in London. I rented this coach to take some of the players to Stratford. We are on the way back to London and have a train to catch Sunday afternoon."

"Well, I wish I could help you. If my grandparents hadn't taken their car we could get you back to Stratford tonight. At least you'd be in a hotel."

"So there is no car?"

"No, I'm afraid not. I have a friend down the road though, she works for my grandparents. Why don't you stay here and I'll go ask if she can help. Maybe she knows a mechanic."

I ran down the road to Mrs. Neep's house and banged hard on her door. She was still up. A light came on in her living room and then on the front porch. She looked out the window and saw that it was me and opened the door.

"Nathan, my dear boy, what are you doing?"

"Mrs. Neeps, there is a whole group of soccer or football players stuck in our drive way. I mean their bus is broken down. They're from Germany. One of them used the phone to call someone to help them, but didn't have any luck. They don't have any way back to Stratford. What should we do?"

"Well, invite them in, get the tea mashed, and count the number of beds ye have."

"You mean, let them stay?" I asked bewildered.

"Well of course! Isn't that whut yer Grandmother would do?"

"Invite them in, get you to it, now. I'll be right down to help."

I rushed away from Mrs. Neeps's door step and flew back down the road.

"Wow, what a slumber party!" I thought.

As I rounded the driveway by the bus, I yelled at a group of players kicking a soccer ball up in the air and keeping it up in rotation between them. "Come on in, guys!" Also motioning with my hand, not knowing how many of them spoke English.

They followed me up to the house where their leader, Gunter, was sitting on the front porch.

"My grandparents' friend said you can stay here at the bed & breakfast. Come on in. You can call someone tomorrow morning to come fix your bus."

The group — almost twenty guys in total — gave out a few cheers in German and followed me inside. I grabbed all four keys to the rooms on the second floor and the key for the room down the hall from *Foxglove*, on the third. I figured those who were lucky got the beds first, the rest would have to fight for the sofa, floors, whatever they could find. I gave Gunter the key to a small private room, *Parnassus*.

"Have you guys had dinner, yet?" I asked Gunter, who

was trying to bring some organization to the loud group.

"No, we've been too busy celebrating in one of the pubs in Stratford. Lunch was the last meal we ate."

"Would your team members want to eat?"

"Now?"

"Well, yes, I could fix something. I've been doing it all summer," I said, pointing upstairs for some of the guys to find their rooms.

"What would you fix us?" Gunter asked.

"You probably couldn't be choosy, we didn't know you were coming. Ordinarily, my grandmother would be putting together a nice German meal for you. She likes her guests to feel at home."

"Anything will be fine, uh, what was your name?"

"Nathan."

"Thanks Nathan, I'll tell the men to come on down and that we'll eat in a while."

I went to the kitchen and began looking through the cooler for something to feed the newest arrivals. In the pantry I happened upon a giant can of sauerkraut, which I opened.

"Me God, what is that terrible odor?" Mrs. Neeps said, rushing into the kitchen behind me.

"Sauerkraut. I found a giant can of sauerkraut in the pantry. Germans like sauerkraut, you know."

"You mean they haven't eaten?

"Not yet. And Gunter, their leader or manager or something, said they were hungry. They haven't eaten since lunch. But they ought to be in a good mood, he said they had been in a pub all evening."

"Won't this just be the dandy evening," Neeps replied. "How many of them are there?"

"I think seventeen or eighteen, almost twenty," I said.

"What are we going to feed them? They can't just eat sauerkraut, even if they are Germans."

"What goes with sauerkraut, Mrs. Neeps?"

"Normally big juicy German sausages or links. Maybe rare roast beef? I don't really know too many Germans."

"There is a giant box of frozen hot dogs, but I don't think they're German," I said, looking in the freezer.

"Let's put them on to boil and we can see what else there might be," Neeps replied.

We searched through the whole kitchen and found almost nothing that might be considered German cuisine. While the hot dogs cooked, there must have been thirty or forty of them in the pot boiling, Mrs. Neeps got a number of frozen loafs of bread out and began slicing them. I found mustard and started taking the stuff to the dining room. I knew Hope would not do this, this away. She would somehow magically pulled together a full German meal in just an hour for these unexpected visitors. But if they were going to eat, it was up to Neeps and me.

Along with bread, hot dogs and sauerkraut, we put out a lot of fruit and cheese, of which there was plenty. Once the table was set I called out on the porch for Gunter to bring in the team. They had been sitting out on the lawn talking about their recent games in London, and how they planned to get back there for, their trip to Germany. The guys were indeed starving but had continued to drink from bottles of German beer they had bought on the way out of Stratford. When they came into the dining room, two of the young men were carrying a case of the beer which had been on the bus.

"Let's eat," Gunter announced to all, "and let's hear it for Nathan and ..."

"Neeps, Mrs. Neeps," the helpful neighbor replied to Gunter.

"Mrs. Neeps for putting this together for us."

The drunken men cheered, sat down at the table and began gobbling down all that we prepared.

"What is this?" One of the men asked holding up one of the wiggly hot dogs, pierced by his fork.

"It's a hot dog. You know, weiner?" I explained.

They all laughed at the shriveled up "weiner" flopping on the end of the team members' fork.

"You are right. This is a weiner," he said changing the ending word into a sarcastic, effeminate sound. "Only a tiny, little British weiner. But we Germans are used to Sausage! Bratwurst! Kochwurst! Big German weiners!" All the men reasserted the players' bragging with German grunting, whooping, and yelling.

"Be friendly," Gunter reprimanded and continued, "we may have beaten England last week in football...," more loud German grunting and jeers interrupting him, "but our British friends have taken us in and are providing us a meal. Be kind."

"Uh, Gunter, I am not British, I am American," I corrected.

That's all they needed. The same guy who had made fun

of the little weiners, now targeted me.

"American, what kind of football do you play in America? Sissy football!" The guy bragged.

The crowd was really getting out of hand. I started worrying about the situation and thinking that I had made a mistake in inviting the group to stay. A player was sent out and more beer was brought in. It seemed as if they must have had a whole German brewery out in the bus.

In time, all the food on the table was gone, even down to the last little British weenee. The size didn't seem to stop them. All the fruit was gone, bread, too. The current rounds of beer were refueling an entire afternoon of partying. I tried to clear food off the table and move empty bottles out to the kitchen. Neeps was also helping. When most of the mess was cleaned up Neeps whispered to me she had to go. She also whispered to Gunter that perhaps he should bring the impromptu party to a close. I thanked the neighbor and she left us, gladly.

Even though I had had the wine a month or so earlier, and several drinks since, I didn't join in this affair. I was afraid that Nanna's house and belongings, might end up destroyed, that I would be blamed, and further damage my mother's relationship with her parents. I was ready for a show down and willing to take a stand.

A third and forth case of beer was brought in and the teammates were only talking in German at this point. Each and every word was accentuated as if it were the most important word in each sentence. Several of the guys got really loud, not in a fighting way, but just bragging it seemed. Their sentences grew shorter and they were obviously doing less listening to each other. And then from their nonverbal messages they seemed to be complaining.

"What was going on?" I thought. Was everything going to fall apart. The dining room table broken into bits and pieces, glass lamps busted, what? The guys were mimicking singers, spouting off words to songs. Now it seemed that they were going to fight. At a point when it seemed as if the whole room were going to explode with the frenzy of seventeen drunken, boisterous German soccer players just coming off a high at wining their tournament I walked around to Gunter, bent over and spoke in his ear.

"What are you're friends talking about. They seem like they are about to kill each other. I am afraid for my grandmother's house. Are things going to be OK?" I asked, sounding upset.

"Oh no, Nathan. They are talking about who their favorite singers are. They are discussing who is the best American singer."

I was relieved, at least somewhat.

"Well, who do they say?" I wanted to know.

"About half the group thinks Lena Horne is the best. The other half feel Elvis Presley is the best. They are wishing they could hear them sing a recording and then decide."

I thought for a minute. I didn't know if Pahpee had any Lena Horne music, but I knew he had Elvis albums. Nanna loved Elvis and would often talk about him and his hips.

I got up from my place at the dining room table and went to the study. The last thing this group needed was more energy, but I was so relieved that they weren't about to fight, even though it sounded like they were, I decided to bring in the record player and some of the Elvis albums.

The guys went crazy when they saw me carrying in the stuff. They helped by taking the albums out of my hands and plugging in the record player. Quickly the group knew what they wanted to hear, *Jail House Rock*. I put on the music and the guys started to sing — out loud — along with Elvis. Their husky, over bearing, athletic, German voices were a great contrast to Elvis's smooth delivery. The entire group knew every English word to the song. Several of them grabbed wooden dining room chairs and began dancing with them on the line, "If you don't have a partner use a wooden chair," right there in Nanna's dining room.

The group roared when the song was finished. Next came, *Love me Tender*. To this, one of the soccer, well OK, football players jumped up on the table, still protectively covered with a table cloth, and sang into a wax candle stick "microphone" he grabbed off the buffet. The rest of the group looked up at him as if they were actually looking at the king himself. On ending of *Tender*, more cheers, more beers.

This went on for over an hour. Some songs were repeated with a different lip-sync star, the group often rising to their feet dancing with each other, on the table, all over the room. The event really turned out to be another international event sponsored by Hope's Croft. American rock 'n roll, German voices, all happening in an olde English dinning room. I was amazed at what I saw and enjoyed the entertainment immensely. So immensely, that I was coaxed up on the table for the last song, *Blue Christmas*.

After one AM in the morning, the last of the beer was gone, empty bottles were strewn everywhere, and the group dropped off from exhaustion. The place was a mess. I locked the front door and just let those who were on the floor stay where they were. I went up to bed and tried to fall asleep. For awhile, the sound of almost two dozen snoring German men, spread over three floors, kept me wide awake. Soon though, thoughts of what a wonderful place Hope's Croft was lured me into a deep sleep, then again, maybe it was the snoring.

In the morning, Gunter called the bus company who sent another bus from Stratford to pick up the team and transport them to London. Gunter thanked me, gave me three one hundred sterling pound bills and said he hoped everything was all right. I told him to be sure and have everyone sign the guest book and that I would have Nanna send him a receipt. Shortly, the group boarded a new bus, a wrecker came to tow away the first bus, and I was left to clean up Hope's Croft.

Mrs. Neeps walked up to the croft shortly there after and together we stripped the sheets off the beds, washed several sinks of dishes and vacuumed the entire B&B. Numerous sacks of trash and beer bottles were taken out. By the middle of the afternoon we had finished cleaning and so we sat down to drink some juice and eat a slice of short bread on the back patio.

"Neeps, thanks for helping me get everything back in shape. Nanna and Pahpee would have been furious had they walked in with it looking like that. They planned on coming home tomorrow afternoon, but you never know," I said.

"Oh, it's just fine. I had nothing else to do, really."

I sat and looked at Mrs. Neeps. She was in her mid-twenties, not unattractive. It did seem from her clothes and small rock house that she probably struggled financially most of the time, just like my mother and me. She was Hope's Croft housekeeper, after all. She was a humble but hard working woman. But is was strange that all summer I had never heard about children or a husband, even though she was called, "Mrs.," so I asked.

"Neeps, do you have any children?"

"Aaugg! Children? Neeps? Nathan you must be joshing ol' Neeps. I don't 'ave any children, probably never will, can't stand them, really. Can't stand them one bit," she said laughingly.

"You don't like *me*?"

"Aaugg, Nathan, you're different. You're almost a grown man. Besides, your not me own."

Being cautious, and sounding concerned, I asked, "Are you married?"

"Aaugg! Me? Neeps married? Nathan you really are joshing me. No. Absolutely not married. Not Neeps."

I laughed at her response which relieved some of the tension. "Well, why do you call yourself, 'Mrs.,' then?" I added.

"Ohhh, Nathan. Neeps was married once. When I was seventeen. But that experience taught me I didn't care for marriage. He was a gutter boy from Bedfordshire. He drank too much and used me like a wet mop, he did. My parents didn't 'ave much use for me so I just left. Moved. Came to Stratford looking for work and a place to live. I heard about

Hope's Croft needing a cleaning lady and was hired. No, marriage is not for Neeps."

"But did you divorce him?"

"Aaugg! No, not one bit. That's why I am 'Mrs. Neeps!,' Can't afford a divorce. Nope. Not one bit of that."

Even though there was a lot of anger in Neeps's voice, there was also a ring of confidence, like she could make it on her own and be jolly proud of the fact. She didn't need men, didn't want one. We sat a little longer, drinking our juice, and resting from several hours of cleaning. She looked straight at me. She looked at me with the same gaze she gave me at her little rock house the night she asked me to take the tins of short bread to Nanna. The looked haunted me. It was as if she wanted to say something to me, but was afraid.

"Neeps, what's wrong? You looked at me as if something's wrong," I said, both curious and concerned.

"Nathan, your mother and Mrs. Briscoe don't get along too well, eh?"

"Not at all."

"Neeps has worked for your grandmother for over five years. She's a fair lady. She doesn't know I am not divorced. I could tell right off she wouldn't go for that kind of shenanigan. Hope Briscoe is straight up. Proper. Maybe, a bit too proper."

"How's that?"

Neeps's voice got lower in tone and volume. She moved over toward me as if to confide, through there wasn't anyone around but me to hear.

"Nathan, my dear friend, I've heard your grandmother

talk about your mother on a number of occasions. See, cleaning help is like 'furniture' to those who are well-off. She talks about your mother because she thinks I have no interest in the conversation. Like I am just one of the dressers we are dusting."

"I understand."

"Mrs. Briscoe has been angry at your mother because of they way she left, which she says was about twenty years ago."

"I don't know the exact date but it was before I was born, which was in 1954. I was born in the United States."

"Your mother, Nathan, and I don't want to hurt you...,"

"No please, please go on."

"Your mother was pregnant, that is according to Mrs. Briscoe. From what I've heard in many one-sided conversations, Mrs. Briscoe was very angry about the whole thing. She often talks about that, "damned service man.""

"Neeps, that's my father. Or was..."

"She felt it was the service...your father?" Neeps asked.

"Yes, my father was an American Army-Air Force service man. He was stationed in London to help train British pilots to fly bombers. They met here, in England."

"But then you're not twenty years old, so how..."

I sighed deeply. "That's what I want to know. Do I have a brother or sister somewhere, here in England, back in the United States? What?"

"Nathan, my dear boy, I don't know that, not one bit. I wish I could tell you, but she has never talked or discussed any grandchildren with Neeps."

"She has made it clear, unknowingly to me, that she was unhappy that your mother was pregnant. She has also mentioned that she had hoped her only daughter would have married a British boy. She could understand your mother's desire to get out of Britain back when the country entered the War. She even said several times, 'Who could blame her? Everyone wanted to leave.' But Mrs. Briscoe could never understand her daughter going off to the United States, permanently, and living where she would almost never see her daughter or grandchildren."

"This is such a mess. And it's a mess that has gone on too long. This is stupid that two grown people are so mad at each other that they live clear across an ocean from one another, not speaking. Not talking...for my whole life! Even longer!"

"Nathan, if one of them would just say they're sorry, I think it would end. If they would give in. Isn't it strange how people are willing to destroy a lifetime of happiness over a few seconds of victory? Pride. It's just like a damned war!"

"Thanks, Neeps, for telling me what you have heard. You are have helped me understand a little more. Somehow my visit has got to bring them together."

"Hope I didn't upset you, love."

"Not one bit, Neeps. Not one bit." I said, as she laughed.

I spent the rest of the day, taking care of the animals which was my responsibility while Nanna and Pahpee were away in London for the weekend. Afterward, I went down to the River Stour for a few jumps off the rope, then back to the Croft. I stopped to get the mail by the road that was delivered on Friday, which I had forgotten to do. There was a stack of letters, among them, another letter from, Siljan.

As usual, the letter started off, "My Dearest Nathan."
I read the first few lines and then realized I wasn't really interested in Siljan anymore. It's not that I wasn't spellbound by her, its just that my thoughts were on trying to bring my family back together. And, if I was going to spend my time romantically involved with anyone, if would be Ginny, though I had put off writing far too long.

Without even completing the letter, I went into the hall bath room, got down on my knees and retrieved several other letters she had sent over the last two months from the hiding space. I placed this newest one with them, and replaced the small bundle back under the sink.

Later, I fixed my own dinner and went to bed early. I laid in bed wondering how I could patch up this family squabble, if not on-going war. I fell asleep wishing for a resolution.

The next morning I awoke to the smell of a traditional English breakfast being prepared. I jumped out of bed and went downstairs wondering what was going on. There was Pahpee and Nanna making breakfast in the kitchen. They had come back very early in the morning and were hungry.

"How was your trip? Is the friend OK?"

"No Nathan, actually he died last evening. We decided to get up early and come back home. Did you make out all right on your own?"

"The place is in order isn't it?" wanting to skirt the possibility of talking too much about the proceedings of Friday evening, but continuing matter of factly, "Oh we did have unexpected guests Friday night. Some soccer, or football players from Germany. Their bus broke down. Neeps came down and we fed them some hot dogs and bread from the freezer. No big deal. There are three, one hundred pound notes in an envelope in the guest book."

They both looked at me astonished.

"See, I told you I could take care of things," I smiled back to them.

I don't believe I'll ever forget how I felt at that moment. It wasn't helping the unexpected Germans, cooking for them, or cleaning the messy house afterwards that made me feel good. It was the look in Pahpee and Nanna's eyes, the surprise that I was able to handle their place of business while they were away. That made me feel great!

❊ ❊ ❊

I turned a page, and there was a photo in the album I had never seen. Apparently Gunter had sent it back to the croft long after I left. It was a photo of me standing on the cloth covered dining room table, surrounded by a bunch of drunken Germans football players. I was using a candle stick as a microphone, singing, I think, *Blue Christmas*.

CHAPTER EIGHT

My new friends,

Words cannot describe the happiness you have brought me during my short stay at Hope's Croft. You are delightful friends that I shall remember affectionately as I return to Lyon, France. Nathan, you are very special. Think about our talks along the Avon as you return to Pennsylvania. You know, my dear son, life is what you make of it, where you make it!

Jean Clarke Montereau

J ean Clarke Montereau. What an individual to know during my last few days at Hope's Croft! He was soft spoken,

French, tall, athletic, and a college professor at the University of Lyon. He was single, by choice, and taught American Studies. He knew almost everything about the United States there was to know. In fact he knew more about the United States than I did, and he wasn't even American.

When John Clarke arrived I was asked to take his things to *Sheep Laurel* on the second floor. The room was much more masculine than the others on the floor and even had its own small library. Mostly, love stories were placed on the shelves in *Sheep Laurel*. I suppose Pahpee felt that if a bedroom was going to have books in it, the books out to be about the happenings of bedrooms.

Pahpee had all the great love stories from literature. A few guests during the summer of '62 checked into *Sheep Laurel* and only came out to eat, and sometimes even skipped that. Love can make a person do some awfully silly things.

I didn't get to talk much to Jean Clarke the first evening he stayed with us. He was very private. But, before bed, Pahpee came up to my room and said Mr. Montereau asked about bicycling to Stratford after breakfast. He had planned to spend the day in Stratford. Pahpee asked me if I would like to go along with him, to show the man the way, and then return by lunch. I agreed and went on to bed.

In the morning, after the traditional English breakfast, I had a lot of traditional English breakfasts that summer, I got two bikes out of the barn and got them ready for the trip. By bicycle the trip was less than two hours. The road to Stratford is narrow and lined with quaint little rock bridges and centuries old farm houses. In the late summer, wild flowers bloom all along the way beside the road. The trip is like a series of English postcards, places that you think are only drawings or paintings, but really do exist.

We rode side-by-side, talking about our various homes and families. Montereau had taught American culture and English at the University for twenty years. Surprisingly, he had traveled to Philadelphia once. Philadelphia was less than an hour from our apartment. He had gone there to study the French and Indian War which began in western Pennsylvania in 1754. Montereau told me that the British had won the war nine years later. Funny, even though I had Pennsylvania history just the proceeding year, I didn't remember the French being in a war there and likewise, I thought the only war we fought against the British was, lost by the British. As I said, Mr. Montereau knew a lot about America. In time, I would discover he knew a lot about me.

The ride to Stratford was leisurely. He even described the ride using the word, leisurely, and explained it came from the French language meaning, "free time." Jean Clarke had a way of informing you about the history of a word or event without making you feel like a complete idiot. He used great care in every word he spoke. Each sentence rolled out of his mouth like words from a well written book.

"The green, rolling pastures are splattered with dollops of white sheep, like smidgens of cream-colored oil paint, Nathan. Their sounds echo off brown stone fences, warning us of the approaching fall," he expounded as we cycled past a meadow of just plain white sheep.

Once in Stratford, I gave Jean Clarke a map Pahpee had

given me and told him I'd be returning to the B&B. Pahpee wanted Mr. Montereau to have his own time and space, I would be in the way.

"I must be on my way back to the croft. Do you need anything else?" I asked.

"You are leaving, so soon? But we have just arrived."

"Pahpee said you would probably want to see Stratford on your own without distractions?"

"Today, I would be lost if not accompanied by your presence. Shall we see Stratford, together, our wheels in tandem? I have authored several Shakespearean articles and you would have an extraordinary tour guide. However, if you must depart, I would understand, but if you would like to know more about Shakespeare, I would be honored to be your teacher."

What do you stay to a man like Mr. Montereau, "Nope, I've gotta go feed the sheep, sorry." I readily admit there was never anyone from the steel mill that talked, thought, or moved like Jean Clarke Montereau. Though he seemed a little quirky, what else was I to say, but yes! I called Pahpee from a pay phone and we were off for a day of tracing William Shakespeare's foot steps.

First, we started at Anne Hathaway's cottage. It was some distance from town and it took a while to ride there, but was worth it. The thatch covered roof and the wild flower gardens were beyond description. Inside, a large hooded fireplace was framed by warming pans used on cold evenings. Surely, they warmed Anne and her beau, William. We passed up the guided tour and strolled through the gardens. Montereau told me fascinating stories of Anne Hathaway and her courtship with William. He explained how Shakespeare went off and left her behind in Stratford for seven years while he worked — and played— in London theatre. After the lecture we rode from Shottery, the tiny community where the house was located, back to Stratford.

In town, Jean Clarke took me by Dr. Hall's home, Hall's Croft. This was the home of Shakespeare's granddaughter and her husband. Out behind the large home was a giant flower garden, manicured meticulously. Jean Clarke and I walked up quietly to an old twisted tree, surrounded by summer flowers and watched a hawk demonstration. The hawk-handler worked with several hawks which would occasionally fly over the garden and return to his arm on command. A small crowd of tourists had gathered to enjoy the demonstration, also.

We grabbed a soda water at a small cafe and then biked to the house were William Shakespeare was born. Jean Clarke told me more fascinating stories about Shakespeare's youth and his family as we strolled through the first floor. We went upstairs and peered out a window, the same window that the great playwright had looked through, and I discovered that many great writers —over several hundred years— had etched their signatures into the glass. I felt Mr. Montereau deserved to have his name etched there also, he seemed so brilliant.

At last, we rode down to the Avon, to a large grassy area covered by giant trees. We pulled sandwiches out of a sack Nanna had packed and sat near the river. White swans came around, looking for handouts and so we obliged. Several long boats, crew boats, or "shells" as Montereau described rowed by, probably students from a nearby school. We ate and I sat thinking about all I was learning on this day from this remarkable stranger who seemed to enjoy sharing stories from history with me.

"You know, Nathan, all places have a history, a story to tell, something to give us for our own understanding."

"I suppose," thinking of my own home town.

"My town of Lyon, in France, has many buildings dating back to the Middle Ages. The old town is on the west bank of the Saone River. It is very beautiful, and old. But we also have many manufacturing plants. We know they are important for our culture, for survival, but sometimes they can be troublesome."

"I understand that. We have several big steel mills at home. They cause a lot of pollution and noise. But without them, there would be very few jobs. My mother depends upon the mills and so do my grandparents there. We live in an apartment behind their house. Sometimes...,"

"Sometimes, Nathan, you wished you lived somewhere else?" He interrupted.

"Yes. But not because of the steel mills. I wish my family was, well closer. My father died in World War II. He was a pilot and he met my mother here in England. He never came back. It seems my mother got pregnant and left England during the War. She was lucky enough to ride a ship to the United States, but it cost her a lot. My grandparents don't seem to care about her anymore."

"Nathan, people have expectations. They place others on pedestals, assuming their behaviors will meet those expectations. In life they often don't. When that happens everyone is disappointed. What can you do to get your mother and your grandparents back together?"

"I don't know. Coming here was suppose to do that. But now, I am leaving soon, in just two days. I've not been successful."

"How is it, my dear boy, you feel you have not been successful?"

"Not once have I had a chance to talk about the problem to either of my grandparents. If we don't talk about it, nothing will ever change."

"My friend, sometimes even talking doesn't put all the pieces back together. Nations fight for years, centuries, and still they can only see boundaries at their feet and not the wide vistas across the mountains. Stop and think, where are the boundaries that separate nations?"

"Well, on the ground, like you say. Maybe a sign on a road. I don't know."

"There are no real boundaries. Your states, back in America, in the south, they are fighting about racism. Some cities have laws, written and otherwise, that keep some citizens from entering, sleeping, working. But where are the boundaries, really. On a piece of paper, a map, in a law book? It is all the same dirt, isn't it? Grass does not grow along the road and then merely stop, saying, 'this is Belgium, can't grow here.' Rivers don't cease to flow from one village to the next, one country to the next. It is all one world. The boundaries, between cultures, between people, are..."

"All in our minds," I completed.

"You are becoming a very smart young man, my boy."

I thought about what Jean Clarke Montereau said, what I said. It seemed so simple. The problem was within us. Within my mother. Within Pahpee and Nanna. It was time to go home. Home to Hope's Croft. And then home, home.

Several evenings later I packed for my trip back to Pennsylvania. I took a special wood box Pahpee had made to carry things home I had bought, or that had been given me: a small wooden elephant "Ganesh" from India given by Mr. and Mrs. Srinivas, a soccer ball from the German football team, a Shakespeare play program from Ginny's trip to Stratford, the big brown paper hat the Venetti sisters had made me, an oversized photo of me with Larry and Lambkin from Pahpee and Nanna, and Mr. Bledsoe's false teeth thoroughly sanitized — he had mistakenly placed them in my shaving kit in the hall bathroom and I hadn't noticed them until after his unexpected and unannounced departure the next day.

On my last morning, I took my things out to the porch and was greeted by two college-aged girls from Amsterdam. They had on backpacks and looked well worn from their travels. They asked if there were any vacancies, I said that they would need to check inside with my grandparents. One stayed outside while the other went in. The one outside introduced herself as Julianne Rijk. She said she and her friend had been "out" all summer and were on their last leg home.

"What is there to do around here?" Julianne asked.

"If you like to swim, there is a great tree down at the river, the River Stour, with a long rope for jumping."

"Sounds fab. Do you do 'hish,'" she asked.

"What?"

"Hish. Hashish. You know compacted grass."

"You mean marijuana?" I asked, in a whisper, looking to make sure no one was coming outside.

"Yeah, man. It is too fine."

"No, no thanks," I replied, I had had enough new experiences for one summer. As we waited for her friend to come out and Pahpee to drive me to the station, I thought what would happen if my proper grandmother and these two college girls collided at Hope's Croft. Perhaps a repeat of the Bledsoe incident. The first girl came out and explained to her friend that the room cost was beyond their depleted budget. The girls would instead hitch a ride into Stratford and look for the youth hostel.

We loaded the car, Nanna came out and surprisingly gave me a hug. How strange. Mr. Montereau, who would be a guest for a few more days, shook my hand and winked at me. Neeps came running up the drive way with a tin of short bread which we stuck in the wood carrying case. She hugged me long and hard and flashed a huge crooked tooth smile.

I got in the front seat of the car, Pahpee was kind enough to let the two girls ride along in the back seat and out the long driveway we drove. For three months, I had waved-off guests from the other end of Hope's Croft driveway. Some I'd never remember, some I'd never forget.

I maneuvered the London trains and made it to the airport. The flight back was long. My mother greeted me at the Philadelphia airport with a hug and a smile. I had no great news for her in solving her difficulties with her parents. But as we drove back into Bethlehem I gave her the following advice:

"You know mom, the only boundaries we have in this world are the ones inside of us. The ones we make up. All else is unimportant. If we can figure out how to remove those imaginary lines of pride, power, and selfishness, conflicts just go away. Why don't you write Nanna and Pahpee and tell them how you feel. Tell them how you feel way down inside."

Our conversation on this topic ended as we crossed over the Lehigh River, going away from our apartment located above my Pennsylvania grandparents' garage. She had planned a surprise for me while I was gone during the summer.

My mother had moved us into an apartment with two bedrooms. She had decided a growing teenager needed more space. She had received a bonus at the mill, for twenty years of service, and that had made it possible. I looked forward to my new home in Bethlehem, and already missed the one I had just left behind, right outside Stratford, England.

❄❄❄

I closed the book marked 1962, and allowed it to drop softly to the hardwood floor beside me in the study of Hope's Croft B&B. The sun had now slipped below the horizon and the last few rays of orange-red light ceased to shine through the round pane of glass in the study window. Out the window, the western sky was an alternating ribbon of rose and purple clouds. The room was darker. As attorney John Hall had said, the electricity had been shut off for some time. It would get dark. He'd be back.

I sat and thought about the guests from the summer of 1962. I thought about all of them, collectively as a group, an experience that had a profound impact on me as a teenage boy, but somehow had never rectified itself in a positive way to bring my family together.

Pahpee had died. Mother had died. I had grown to middle age. And now, just a few weeks earlier Nanna had passed away quietly in a nursing home, six years after she closed the doors for the last time. She had died without me knowing that she was even still alive.

The pages of the guest book had captured my attention for several hours as I sat in the comfortable leather chair. The same chess pieces, which had been the object of my playfulness with Ginny Allbritton, stood quietly at attention, all in their proper rows, just across the room on a game board that hadn't been moved in years.

The guest book now on the floor, all the guest books, almost forty years of them, had been so carefully saved. Saved as a monument to Hope Briscoe, her husband, and their many guests...which included me. If she had just had the opportunity to know my father, had he not died, I know they would have liked each other. After all he was a hero. Hope liked me. She would have liked him. She smiled when I explained how I had "commanded the ship" for the soccer players while she and Pahpee were in London. She hugged me the day I left in August 1962. How unfortunate it is that we sometimes fail to see the significance of insignificant actions, which distort the love we should show one another.

A knock came from the front door. It was John Hall.

"Mr. Bradbury, are you here?"

"In here John, in the study."

"Sorry to be delayed, Chap. During my meeting an emergency occurred at a piece of property I manage. A big white swan got tangled in a wayward clothes line. The guests at the house were horrified. We did manage to undo the bird and set her back, free to scurry about in the Avon. All's well, now."

"John, I've been looking at...," I started, but was interrupted by the little youthful man.

"Nathan, I stopped by the office of an associate and picked up a real estate sign. I know you wish to dispose of the property as quickly as possible. I also brought a blank listing agreement for you to sign, which I'll pass along to the agent. He also gave me his business card. You may want to call him."

"John, have a seat."

"It is dark, my friend."

I am sure there is a candle in the dining room. I do want to talk with you. Wait just a moment."

There was indeed a candle in a holder on the buffet. Matches in the drawer right below. I placed the candle on the fireplace mantle in the study which allowed light to be reflected in a mirror above the fireplace. I sat back down.

"John, I want to keep Hope's Croft. I don't wish to sell it.

I want to move to Stratford and re-open the B&B. What do you think?"

"But you are from Pennsylvania. You don't live here."

"I know, but I want to. Can I do that?"

"Well, yes, an American citizen can own a business in England, but you would have to remain a US citizen, I suppose. You wouldn't want to become a Brit would you?"

"Maybe, I don't know. I do know I don't even want to go back home. I plan to call back and quit my job at the steel plant. I will have my apartment manager gather my things and put them in storage. What do you think? Do you think I can pull this off?"

"Nathan, you can do anything you set your mind to. You have plenty of money, zero mortgage, and apparently an interest in this project. Let's go celebrate! I'll take you out to eat. Where would you like to eat? What kind of food do you like?"

"I've never tried Indian. You said there was one near the Avon, earlier."

"Let's be off. Indian it is."

We locked the big front door of Hope's Croft and headed out to Hall's convertible Fiat. In minutes we drove up to one of several Indian restaurants in Stratford. Seated inside, I allowed John to order for me as I knew nothing about Indian food. He ordered. We talked about legal arrangements and I poured out my impromptu plan to reestablish Hope's Croft.

Soon our spicy Indian food was brought by a beautiful young dark skinned girl with a jeweled bendi on her forehead.

"Uh, just a minute, can you tell me what, 'Namastay,'

means? Did I say it correctly?"

"Yes sir, it is pronounced just the way it sounds; Na-ma-stay. It is the official, unofficial greeting for good-bye and hello in India, spoken mostly by those living in southern India. But it means much more than simply, hello. It means, 'From my heart, to your heart, I wish you only the best today!'" All three of us looked at each other and then, almost in unison said, "Namastay!"

C H A P T E R N I N E

The next few days I began lining up painters and carpenters. The barn needed work, the fence out front was falling down, and some of the interior woodwork needed attention. Everything was to be repainted. With all the activity neighbors began to stop by and ask what was happening. Just a few days after work began, I was pulling early spring weeds out of the back flower beds. I was having trouble pulling some very stubborn under growth and heard an older voice behind me.

"Aaaug, ye going to 'ave to pull a bit harder to get those stubborn weeds out," a woman, about sixty years of age, commanded.

I turned and was astonished to see, Neeps. An older, much older, but never-the-less, Mrs. Neeps.

"Neeps?" I said cautiously.

"Ye, and who might you be?"

I'm Nathan, Neeps. Remember, Nathan Bradbury. Nathan from the summer of 1962. Hope's grandson, Nathan.

At the last urging she figured it out and rushed to me. The lady still had a powerful hug. After a hug she placed her hands on my shoulders and looked right at me.

"You are, you are Nathan. Me gosh, what are you doing here. I've not seen ye for, for...,"

"Thirty-five years, thirty-five years, Neeps," helping her with the measurement of time.

"You are all grown up, Nathan."

"Grown up and beyond, Neeps."

"Why are you here? Are you...?"

"Yes! As you know, Hope passed away last month. Attorney John Hall contacted me and, after looking over the place, I've decided to move here, and re-open Hope's Croft. What do you think?"

"I think it's bloody wonderful!"

"I do too, bloody wonderful!" I added, trying to mimic her cockney accent. "Want a job?"

"Nathan, I 'aven't worked for Hope's Croft in, well since 1990 when Hope fell ill. She had a spell one weekend and never came back. Been in a nursing home in Stratford ever since. I 'ave taken care of Hope over the years. Take her fresh shortbread every few weeks, I 'ave."

"You 'ave a new job, Mrs. Neeps," I said, still carrying on my weak cockney speech and continuing, "I'll pay ye double, what ever ye last job paid."

"Well, I am a bank president, now Nathan, so..."

We both broke up in laughter.

"Job accepted, Nathan...Nathan..." Neeps struggled.

"Bradbury, it's been a long, long time," I said, my voice calming down and lowering some, holding her by the hand. I went in and got the guest book from 1962 and we visited for many hours, looking at all the people and laughing about the Germans. She agreed to come the next day and help me "a bit" as she put it with some cleaning. The evening passed.

Early the next morning I started pulling all the guest books off the shelves and placing them carefully in boxes I had retrieved in town in my new wheels. (A few days earlier John Hall told me about a second hand pickup truck which I bought, that seemed necessary for the task ahead.) On the top shelf, behind the books, was a small bundle of envelopes, secured with a rubber band. The second I touched the bundle, the dried-out rubber band snapped. I pulled the stack of envelopes off the shelf and looked at the addresses. I was amazed, the first three were from "Christina Siljan."

I opened the top letter and was shocked to find it to be the first letter she had sent me. My first "love letter." There were others from her, some opened, one still sealed. I opened the latter and discovered that she had decided, since I had failed to answer her correspondence, that our relationship was over and she would no longer be writing.

The former Swedish model would be in her sixties now, I wondered where she was, what she was doing. And then it hit me, I had hidden the letters under the sink, in the third floor bathroom. How did they get in the study, on the top shelf?

I ran upstairs to the floor hall bathroom and knelt down on the floor. I looked up at he pedestal sink where it joins the wall. No hole! Covered over, maybe by a plumber? Pahpee? He must have found the letters and placed them together in the study.

"My gosh, had he read the letters?" I wondered. "What did he think of me? She was obviously writing to someone she loved. I re-read all the letters and was shocked to find, "I miss us holding each other, kissing you, Nathan." Yep, he knew.

I flipped through more envelopes. The next one after Siljan's was addressed to Pahpee, and the return address was from my mother, in Bethlehem. I opened and read the letter dated December 20, 1962. The words from my mother were direct. She said she wanted to mend her relationship with her parents. That while she understood their unhappiness over her unplanned pregnancy, it did after all, end with a miscarriage. She felt that too many years were slipping by and it was important to, "remove the boundaries," that existed between them. She said, at the end, "I'm sorry."

I stood looking at the letter that I had never heard about. A letter that had apparently never evoked a response from Nanna or Pahpee in spite of its sincerity. Even mother's apology, following the advice that Mr. Montereau had given me, did not move my grandparents off center. What anger they must have felt toward us, me. Was it also the photo of the German party, sent long after my summer visit? Me on the dining room table of their house, a candle from the buffet in my hand singing wildly, drunks in the background? Was it the letters from Siljan, exposing our illicit affair in the barn, she twice my age? How would I ever know?

My mother had tried, after all, but nothing in return happened. For so long nothing happened. I did think that, until I flipped to the following envelope. It was addressed to my mother in Bethlehem, to our *old* garage apartment. The apartment that belonged to my dad's parents. The return address showed Pahpees name and Hope's Croft address in the upper left corner. Right across the front of the envelope, now in faded pale red ink was a Bethlehem, Pennsylvania postal stamp, "RETURN TO SENDER, NO LONGER AT THIS ADDRESS JAN. 2, 1963."

I sat down in the leather chair, dropping all the other letters to the floor. The envelope was still sealed. Sealed for thirty-five years, never opened once it had been mailed by Pahpee and returned, never reaching its intended destination. My impulse was to tear open the envelope quickly, to read the words of response from my grandfather, to my mother. I was fearful of doing so. Would the letter be just another emotional whacking for the misdeeds of a mother and her son? Would I regret for the *next* twenty years hearing the thoughts of my grandfather expressed *post mortem* to his grandson, without an opportunity to discuss? To hell with it! Fear that is. I slid a stained finger nail under the flap, opening the yellowing paper. Out came the following one-page letter:

My dear daughter —

How we enjoyed having Nathan stay with us last summer. He is such a fine young man. He helped each day at Hope's Croft, working hard to be a perfect guest, a perfect grandson. You must be very proud of him. He is a tribute to your sole guidance and love.

We feel very guilty at having thrown up fences that have separated us for so long. Your letter is correct, "The only boundaries that exist are the ones in our minds."

Somehow, we hope we can erase the years of heartache, and that you and Nathan will come visit soon.

Love always —
Your Father

They forgave each other! He knew. She didn't. I do, now. We had moved from the apartment at the end of the summer right after my return. The apartment must have stayed vacant or new renters simply gave the letter back to the carrier, and it was returned. However it happened, my mother and I never got the word. I will always believe that even though she never heard from my grandfather, my mother was at peace in asking for forgiveness. That's what counts.

I picked up all the letters and placed them in the guest book marked 1962, and took them to my room, the bedroom used by Nanna and Pahpee on the first floor at the back of the house. The brass name plate still announcing, *Geranium*.

Later in the day, the painters came and the project to once again rekindle Hope's Croft spirit into a place of international connectiveness was on the way. Neeps helped in planning meals and buying new linens, boy did she have fun with that responsibility. I hired an agency in Stratford to send out brochures announcing the re-opening in August. I supplied them with addresses from the guest books. Most people had listed them when they checked out and made their comments. Nanna had also kept an extensive address list of her guests, most repeating customers. Brochures were sent out to all those, as well.

In only weeks the mailbox was full of reservations from old friends. The phone never stopped ringing. Neeps was employed as a full time staff person and she had the opportunity to hire her own cleaning employees. A chef was added and the guests, old and new, arrived nonstop. The Venetti twins wrote and hoped to come visit though each were having some health problems at age sixty seven. They had remembered the "swim" even after all these years and were still amused by it.

By the middle of the fall season, Hope's Croft was a very busy place. The week before Christmas, however, there were no reservations. Most people were with their families and folks don't "pleasure" travel as much. During this time I had planned to fly back to Pennsylvania to get my possessions out of storage. I had to rent another apartment, however, to serve as a permanent residence, as I never relinquished my US citizenship. I had planned to head back on December 20 and was just finishing up from hosting a group of New Zealanders. The phone rang just as the group was departing for their trip home. On the other end of the line a voice said, "My name is Virginia Patterson, would you have a room available for the next few evenings?"

Using a British accent I had begun to try — and taking a hint from the college acting students I met on the airplane — I responded, "Actually, we had planned to close for a few weeks and then re-open in January."

"I see."

"Are you stranded?"

"Well yes, I came to Stratford hoping to stay in town but every 'No-vacancy' sign is out. Are they all full?"

"No, no, no. People hang those out when they don't want to be disturbed. A lot of B&B owners have family in town and need the rooms for holiday."

"Oh, I see."

"If you are in a bind, I could let you stay a few days, at

least until I head out of town, come on by. Do you know where we are located?"

"I have a brochure and will have a taxi bring me out. I'm in the tourist office in Stratford."

"Good, see you shortly,"

I hung up and went up stairs to make up one of the rooms, *Columbine*, the white wicker room and closest to the stairwell. I had the room together in no time and flew back down stairs just as a knock came from the front door. I pulled open the door and turned immediately back to the register in a business-like manner, I was tired and had looked forward to not having guests.

"Just sign here, please," turning to see a beautiful blonde haired woman, in her late forties.

"Thanks, I really did need a place to stay for a few nights," the attractive woman signed her name and town: "Virginia Patterson, Gosford, Australia." I looked down at the signature and then back up at the face which looked so youthful...not at all a woman the age of, forty-eight?

"Ginny?"

"Well, yes, Virginia, normally," she responded squinting as she looked at me.

"Ginny who stayed at Hope's Croft in 1962?" Upon my question she looked at me very curiously.

"Uh, Nath...Nathan?

"Yes! Yes! Oh, yes!"

"My God!"

Then, a tall middle-aged man from Bethlehem, Pennsylvania and a very attractive Australian from a little fishing town hugged tightly in the entry hall of Hope's Croft.

We spent the next few hours talking about our lives, our disappointments, our dreams unfulfilled. Her recent divorce. My lifetime of singleness. How we felt about each other back when we were youngsters.

I prepared a wonderful meal for Ginny and we visited in the kitchen, drinking wine, getting to know one another again. After a candle lit meal in the dining room, and more wine, we danced to music playing on the same old player that had belonged to Pahpee and Nanna, using many of the same songs they had enjoyed. Later, I went with Ginny to *Foxglove*, instead of *Columbine*, and we made love all night and into the morning, just as the sun broke over the horizon, spilling golden morning light through the round glass in the window, making a reflection high on the wall. We laid there, drifting off to sleep as the reflection of the sun, focusing in a clear sharp pattern, climbed up the wall in my favorite room of Hope's Croft B&B.

ACKNOWLEGEMENTS

Thanks to the following for believing in me, helping to prepare the layout, and for understanding the word "no" does not exist: William Clark, The Vines Agency, Kristal, Daniel and Kirk Stafford, Don Bagwell, Bill Stratton, and friends at Digital Impact, Sara Zimmerman, Jason Pritchett, Jason Blackburn, Doris Holbrook and friends at Wal-Brook, artist Chris Bazley, Dr. Lisa Hodges-Lumpkin, Dr. Curtis Bradford, Dr. Vijaya Kandala, Anne Cash, Waka Osaki, Renee Grant, Lores Hauck, John, Kelly and Sara Beth Fede, Chris and Angie Wright at Alderminster Farm, Stratford upon Avon.

ABOUT THE AUTHOR

R.D. Stafford is a college professor of theatre arts in Georgia. In addition to teaching and writing, he conducts seminars on teamwork and leadership. He is the author of *The Funeral Club*, a weekend novel situated in a rural, southern funeral home and operated by five senior-aged women. The book was selected by the South Carolina Center for the Book for several Movable Feasts, raising funds to improve literacy in South Carolina. It was also selected for inclusion in the Greenville, South Carolina Celebrate Reading Festival in 1997. The novel has been featured as an "author-signing" event by the South East Booksellers Association (SEBA) during their 1997 annual conference in Mobile, Alabama. He has also published articles featuring interviews he conducted with Arthur Miller, Edwad Albee, and Frank Rich. Dr. Stafford and his family live near the Blue Ridge Mountains and enjoy sports, fine arts activities, cookouts, and traveling.